MAD LOVE

HEARTS ARE WILD

RHIAN CAHILL

RHIAN CAHILL

Mad Love
Hearts Are Wild Book 3
Copyright © 2019 Rhian Cahill
ISBN: 978-1-925375-29-9
Electronic Edition
Copyright © 2016 Rhian Cahill
Edited by Kelli Collins
Cover by Valerie Tibbs of Tibbs Design

This is a work of fiction. Names, places, characters and incidents are the product of the author's imagination and are fictitious. Any resemblance to actual persons, living or dead, events or establishments is solely coincidental.

For more information visit:
www.rhiancahill.com

*For Mari and Erin. Because no matter what, you've got my back.
And for Kristin. Where would we be without our lunch and
dinner dates?
Mr.C, what can I say. I'm here because you believe.*

TOBY MORELAND LEANED against the wall outside the principal's office and smiled.

How many times over the years had he found himself here?

If he asked his mother, she'd answer with a resounding 'too many'. Of course, these days she didn't get a phone call and he wasn't in trouble.

A tight female voice drifted into the hall. "You cannot believe Mr. Moreland is a suitable option?"

Toby's muscles tensed. Okay, maybe he *was* in trouble.

"Ms. Keibler. Madison—"

"Don't attempt to gain my agreement by using the familiarity of first names, *Mr. Richardson*."

"Look, I understand where you're coming from." The principal's voice held a hint of frustration, a touch of irritation—even a little defeat.

"I don't think you do. This is a serious educational endeavor and the students need to know they can rely on those in charge to deliver the necessary time and knowledge."

"Mr. Moreland is qualified—"

"His skills on the sports field *do not* translate to the classroom."

Toby pushed off the wall. Time to make an entrance. Plastering on a smile, he rapped his knuckles on the doorframe and plunged into what would no doubt be a charged encounter.

"Hey, Ted." He nodded at his friend and boss as he took a seat in front of Ted's desk. Settled, Toby acknowledged the irritated woman standing behind the chair to his right. "Ms. Keibler."

She responded with a brisk nod, but with a stubborn lift of her chin, refused to make eye contact or utter a word.

To hide his grin, Toby faced their boss and asked, "What's this special project you need help with?"

Beside him, Madison huffed. "I can't agree to this, Mr. Richardson."

Ted frowned at her. "You've got no choice. Toby is the only one who might be available and holds the necessary license to drive the bus, but if you feel you can't handle it, we could postpone or cancel."

From the corner of his eye, Toby saw Madison's spine jerk ramrod straight as though someone had shoved a hot poker up her ass. He ducked his head and smiled at Ted's tactic. She was bound to agree now, because Madison Keibler didn't strike him as the type to resist a challenge. And their boss had not only challenged her ability to do whatever this project was, he'd challenged her professionalism and held the threat of cancellation over her too.

Triple whammy.

Madison wouldn't allow her 'serious educational endeavor' to be cancelled. He'd never seen a more dedicated teacher. At times he thought she was *too* devoted to her job.

Over the six years he'd worked at the prestigious private high school, Huntington College, Toby had seen Ted use this method to gain a teacher's cooperation many times. Nine times out of ten it worked. That tenth time usually involved Toby, and he never let himself be manipulated by anyone. Although, he more often than not agreed to Ted's requests.

Best to know all the details before he jumped in to help; he still had no clue what it was they were discussing. "So what's up?" he asked.

"The scholarship class is scheduled for an overnight excursion and needs two teachers to supervise. It's Ms. Keibler's class, and she had Grant lined up, but he's come down with a stomach flu and can no longer go." Ted glanced at her quickly before returning his gaze to Toby's. "I realize it's short notice but they need a second teacher to accompany them on the trip."

"How short?" Toby asked.

"Tomorrow," Ted answered. "But it's only the one night."

"Sure. Count me in." He had the time. Besides, he had every intention of being Madison's partner for this excursion even if he had to rearrange a few things. He'd wanted closer contact with the woman since she'd joined the faculty at the beginning of the year and this was the perfect opportunity to get it. "What do I need to do?"

"Madison has organized everything." Ted pushed a folder across his desk. Tapped the top. "Details are in here."

Toby picked up the thick binder and flicked through it, quickly skimming the pages to determine the input needed from him. He was stunned at the depth of her organization. She'd laid out the activities and objectives for every hour of the excursion. Including the bus ride there and back. Dedicated didn't begin to describe Madison's work ethic.

The urge to needle her—to get under her skin and break through that icy façade—inched up his spine and proved too hard to resist. "You know, Ted, if Ms. Keibler isn't up to it, I can handle this on my own."

"I'm perfectly capable of doing my job," she snapped.

Repressing a smirk, he glanced up to find Madison glaring at him and Ted shaking his head.

"No can do. School policy requires two teachers on off-campus excursions, and besides, it's overnight and a mixed group. Ten boys. Ten girls. We need male and female supervision," Ted explained.

Toby nodded at Ted then looked Madison over. She stood, fingers curled around the back of the chair next to him, her slender digits pressing into the padding under her tight grip. Her body was rigid, and deep lines marred her brow and bracketed her mouth. Her displeasure with the situation was obvious. Even a blind man would feel the tension radiating off her.

He wasn't going to let her annoyance make him back off though. His fascination with getting a reaction from this woman grew with every second he spent with her. "Great. We'll have dinner tonight and go over the details," he said with the smile he knew won over most people—particularly those with two X chromosomes.

She looked down her nose at him and ice dripped from her voice. "That won't be necessary. You don't need to do anything more than show up."

He wanted to laugh at her attempt to exclude him while including him but he held himself in check. She wouldn't appreciate the humor in their current positions.

He'd approached Madison at the start of the year—he and every other single male on the school's payroll—and while she'd been polite, she left no doubt she wanted nothing to do with her male colleagues outside of school. None of the females either, according to Melanie in the English department. Madison kept to herself, only interacting with the rest of the staff when necessary.

Huntington's faculty was a tightknit group that often

socialized after school hours. As a whole, they'd worked together for a few years. Well, except for Madison Keibler. She was a new addition. Last year, when Gordon Rodgers tripped midway through the final term and broke his hip, he'd required a hip replacement and decided to take early retirement.

Enter prim, proper, schoolmarm-ish Madison Keibler.

She reminded Toby of someone out of the eighteen hundreds. Back when teachers were required to be spinsters. At least that's what she made him think of, with her long, dark skirts and starched white blouses buttoned up to her chin. The hair pulled ruthlessly into a bun low on the back of her head didn't help the look either. She couldn't be any older than late twenties but she behaved as though she were in her fifties.

Straitlaced and standoffish. Cool. Like butter wouldn't melt in her mouth. Actually, that shit would probably freeze solid.

It made Toby want to ruffle her. Peel away those don't-touch outer layers and see what was hidden beneath. He had a feeling she'd surprise him.

He liked surprises.

Liked them very much.

MADISON REFUSED to look at the man beside her. She was sure he'd overheard her objections to him accompanying her and waited on tenterhooks for him to call her on it.

Ted was right. All that was required were male and female teachers to supervise, so Tobias Moreland could do the job. She just didn't want him to partner her on this trip.

Something about him set her nerves twitching. She had no idea what it was. He just annoyed her. His whole Mr. Cheery persona rubbed her the wrong way. No one could be that care-free and get their job done—do it well—and Madison believed education was a serious business that required dedicated individuals to perform the job properly.

Her parents had taught her the importance of learning at an early age, and while she might have been a little envious of her peers and the time they spent away from books and libraries, she believed the sacrifices were worth it.

Not that she was as strict as her parents when it came to studying, but she did believe learning didn't finish at three in the afternoon when the school bell rang, signaling the end of formal lessons for the day. Good marks required commitment to study in and out of the classroom.

She knew Moreland's type. They coasted through with minimum grades to pass and spent too much time on frivolous things such as sport and parties...women. Very few individuals succeeded at professional sport and by all accounts, he'd failed, like hundreds of others searching for fame and fortune. Besides, as far as she was concerned, there was nothing special about using a natural talent to make your way through life.

No. True success should be earned, not given.

"We're set then? You'll be ready to leave tomorrow morning at eight?" Ted asked.

Madison eyed the principal and wondered if she'd managed to get on the wrong side of him. She might have a strong opinion about the skill level of the Personal Development, Health and Physical Education teacher but she hadn't been offensive. She'd only put forward the facts as she saw them. Teaching boys to play Rugby League or Union or whatever other brutish sport the PDHPE department deemed acceptable, didn't qualify as education as far as she was concerned.

"I'll be ready." She would bite the bullet—and her tongue— and spend the necessary time with Tobias Moreland but no more. "I'd like to pack the bus with our equipment at seven before the students arrive."

Tobias shook his head. "No can do. Got training."

Of course he did. "Then how do you expect to be ready to leave at eight?"

Long seconds passed without him saying a word. He just studied her through slumberous laughing eyes.

"Well? When do you suggest we organize the equipment?" Exasperation was beginning to take hold, her voice rising slightly with her inability to control her growing frustration.

He smiled up from his slouched position in the chair. "I've got training right after school today but we can do it after that. Around six. Unless you've got a hot date."

Madison narrowed her eyes. Was he fishing for personal information? Why? "Not this evening." And why did she answer him?

"Good." He surged to his feet, all six feet two of solid muscle towering over her—crowding her. She had to fight the urge to retreat from his overwhelming presence. "Let's say six thirty to be sure training's finished. We'll grab dinner afterwards."

"What?"

"Dinner. Tonight. After we load the bus. You can go over the information. Give me the key points of the excursion—the aims, what you hope the students will accomplish." He lifted the folder in his hand and gave it a shake. "Meet you in the car park at six thirty. Catch you later, Ted."

Before Madison could open her mouth to argue, Tobias had left the room taking the folder with him, and, she was fairly certain, all the oxygen. She turned to face Ted. Her jaw worked, her tongue moved, but nothing came out until she utter two words she was one hundred percent certain she'd never spoken before. "I'm confused."

And she was. Did she agree to have dinner with Tobias Moreland?

Ted was busy tapping away at his keyboard and didn't answer right away. When he did, Madison still wasn't sure what was going on.

Absently glancing up while shuffling papers around his desk, Ted said, "Thanks. I hated the idea of cancelling the trip and disappointing the class."

Right. Her students.

This excursion was a fun hands-on way to supplement their education about one of the country's famous landmarks and it would be a travesty if it were canceled. They'd worked extremely hard over the previous months on the history behind the Quarantine Station and it would definitely be a disappointment to them.

And her.

She forced a smile. "Of course."

The end of lunch bell rang.

"That's my cue to head to class," she murmured.

"Thanks again, Madison." Ted returned to pecking at his keyboard with two fingers.

"Right. Okay. I'll...go then." Madison left Ted's office confused and a little flummoxed. She understood the gist of what had happened in the last few minutes, she just wasn't sure *how* it had happened. Her reasons for Tobias's unsuitability had been solid and yet they'd gotten her nowhere. She'd be spending the next two days with a man she could barely tolerate.

She might not be looking forward to working alongside Tobias but she couldn't deny her excitement over exploring and spending the night in one of Sydney's most haunted group of buildings. And nothing thrilled her more than watching young minds discover new things.

The group of teenagers had embraced this section of the history syllabus with such enthusiasm and curiosity she couldn't wait to see them walk the buildings and compound— see through their own eyes the places they'd read about. For their benefit, she'd tolerate her unwanted colleague.

Although it was a shame her anticipation marched hand in hand with the unfamiliar agitation she experienced whenever she saw—or thought about—Tobias Moreland.

2

TOBY SWUNG the door of the storage shed closed, leaned his shoulder into it and gave a good shove. Metal scraped across concrete and he put his full weight against the door to force it those final few inches. They needed to do something about the equipment shed. A new one would be preferable but he'd be grateful for a working door. One that didn't threaten bodily harm whenever someone tried to close it.

As if by some karmic cue, the solid steel panel sprang back and slammed into him, almost knocking him off his feet. "Shit."

"Whoa. We got it."

Two bodies—one either side of him—combined their weight and strength with his to wrestle the door into submission. A few grunts, some scrabbling feet and a heavy clank later, the lock engaged and the door stayed in place.

Taking a breath, Toby stepped back. "Thanks guys." He chose to ignore the fact he swore in front of two of his students. Best to not bring it up. Besides, he'd heard far worse coming from their mouths on the footy field.

"No worries, Mr. Moreland." Jim Landry, Huntington's

star five-eighth, bent to pick up his backpack. Straightening, he added, "It's the least we could do after you helped us with our English essays."

"Yeah. Thanks sir." Andy Sturgis shouldered his bag. "I'd never pass if you didn't take the time to walk me through it."

Toby smiled. "You'd do fine. You just need to stop *thinking* it's too hard. Half the time you talk yourself out of doing well."

Andy ducked his head and shuffled his feet with a mumbled, "Thanks."

For a senior, the kid was a little lacking in self-confidence, except on the football field. There, Andy overflowed with confidence.

Toby clapped them both on the back to nudge them on their way. "Go on. Get out of here. I'll see you in the morning."

Toby watched them head across the field towards the school's rear gate. At this time of day the entrance would be locked, but both boys knew the code to open the gate after hours. Being on the school's League team meant they were on school grounds outside normal operating times in the mornings and early evenings during the footy season.

Speaking of the time...

He glanced at his watch. Ten to seven.

"*Fuck.*"

He was supposed to meet Madison twenty minutes ago. Racing around the shed, he bypassed the most direct route— through the building—for the fastest. The school should be deserted by now but there was a chance one or two people were still inside and he wasn't about to get caught running in the halls. He'd done enough of that as a teenager.

Sprinting the length of the gym, he took the corner wide in an effort to lose as little speed as possible and pumped his legs harder.

Dammit. She was going to be pissed.

His runners lost traction as he flung himself around the final corner and out into the car park. Small pieces of gravel shot out from under his feet as he fought to stay on them and keep moving forward. The school's bus was at the far end, near the admin building, and at least a hundred meters away yet. There were only a couple of cars left in the lot so Toby had an unobstructed view of the bus.

And Madison Keibler, trying to load one of the school's large lockboxes into the rear luggage compartment.

"Hey!" She didn't hear his shout—or chose to ignore it—and continued to struggle with the thing. "Dammit." He dug deeper and gained a bit more speed.

From ten meters out, he saw it happen. The side of the box clipped the edge of the doorframe and rebounded into Madison. Instead of letting go and jumping out of the way, she tried to control the oversized load.

"Jesus." The word exploded on a rush of air as Toby collided with Madison's back. He flung his arms around her and groped for the box.

"What—?" Smashed between him and their precariously tilting cargo, Madison yelped in pain.

"Hang on." He tried to get a better grip so he could shove the lockbox into the back of the bus. Angling to the left, he cleared the doorframe and propelled the box inside.

Although his efforts to keep them from falling were useless, because Madison took exception to being pressed against him and threw her arms out as she spun around.

He tightened his hold as he lost his balance and in the next heartbeat, Toby found himself flat on his back, gasping for breath, with a flailing Madison in his arms.

"Let me go," she screeched in his ear.

Her elbow connected with his ribs knocking the last of the air from his lungs. Knees and feet bashed into his legs, the former coming perilously close to unmanning him, and the latter delivering sharp pain to both his shins. He'd be wearing bruises tomorrow.

"Easy." He tried to grab her arms, pin her legs with his, but she was like the Tasmanian Devil, whirling around frantically. If she kept it up she'd hurt herself. It was too late to stop her from hurting *him*. "Madison!"

She stopped. Sucked in a breath. Her breasts pressed into him and one thigh rested against his cock, which in spite of the recent scuffle and narrow escape from injury, was showing interest in the womanly curves cradled in his arms. "Tobias?"

"Yeah." He breathed in and out slowly, willing his body to behave.

"Oh." She sagged against him, sending all sorts of interesting ideas through his head—the one on his shoulders *and* the one in his pants. "I thought..."

"What?" He frowned. "That I was attacking you?"

"Yes. No. Not you." Madison palmed his shoulders and pushed up, causing her leg to press into his groin with more pressure. There was no way she could miss his reaction to holding her close. She looked down at him with wide eyes for long seconds before saying in a wobbly voice, "I didn't know who'd grabbed me."

"But you thought someone was attacking you?" Toby shook his head clear of lustful thoughts and focused on the conversation. "Jesus, woman, you're in a secure parking lot."

"I...well..." She licked her lips, drawing his gaze, and Toby felt that small action in his balls.

Her face was flushed red and strands of hair floated around her head where they'd come loose from her bun. It was the most disheveled he'd seen her. Toby imagined she'd look similar after an orgasm. His body tightened in response to the new images playing through his mind. Definitely no way she was missing the hard ridge poking her leg now.

"Um..." She caught the right side of her bottom lip in her teeth and sent his blood pressure soring. Blinking slowly several times as if she were in a trance, Madison stared at him with confusion swirling in her gaze. "I..."

"Do you need help getting up?" Not that he wanted her to get up. Toby would be happy to lie here with her spread over him all damn day but he figured once she got her wits about her, she'd be in a hurry to move.

"Oh!" Her eyes opened comically wide and the dark brown color made him think of melted chocolate. "Sorry." With exaggerated care, she untangled herself and climbed to her feet.

Trying to drag his mind out of the gutter and force his body to behave, he rolled to the side and stood. Brushing the gravel and dirt from his clothes, he resolutely ignored the hard-on in his shorts. With Madison no longer in his arms, the lust fog cleared from his brain enough for him to remember the small cry of pain she'd emitted as they'd collided. "Did I hurt you?" he asked.

She glanced around, her hands twisting together in front of her.

"Madison?" He took a step closer. "Are you hurt?"

"Oh. No." Her hands broke apart and smoothed down the sides of her skirt, bringing his attention to the way the material had rucked up her legs to reveal slender thighs.

Her skin looked silky-smooth and his fingers twitched with the need to reach out and touch. Heat washed over him. Shit. He really needed to rein in his desire for this woman. It was becoming more potent by the second. Swallowing, he ran his tongue over his lips then cleared his throat. "Ah, okay. Good." He nodded.

She gave him a tight smile and turned away.

It didn't take a genius to work out she was dismissing him. She had this way about her; she wasn't rude or aggressive, but she conveyed her feelings perfectly without saying a word. For someone who used an economy of words, Madison spoke nonstop with her body and expressions.

When she tried to move the box again, Toby darted forward. "Here. Let me do that."

"I'm fine, thank you."

Her prim tone, the clipped words, shouldn't get him hot. Actually, nothing about her should get him hot. She was the opposite of his type. He went for warm, outgoing, confident, independent... Okay; in some ways she was his type, she definitely had the confident and independent down pat.

"I know you're fine but I'm offering to help anyway."

"Suit yourself." She stepped out of the way and crossed her arms over her chest.

Lord, even the haughty way she held herself got his engine revving.

He wanted her. More than he'd wanted any woman since he'd been an adolescent teeming with hormones.

He'd have to be careful though. This woman wouldn't be easy to win over. She had walls surrounding her. Walls on top of her walls. Except Toby had a feeling they weren't of her making. Since she'd joined the faculty, he'd caught fleeting glimpses of yearning, sadness in her eyes. He may have imagined them but he didn't think so. There were emotions lurking in her gaze he wanted to explore.

She'd barely given him the time of day and he possibly bordered on stalkerville with the way he'd watched her in the last few months, but there was this pull he couldn't seem to ignore. It was sick and probably made him a masochist or something, but the more she telegraphed her dislike, the closer to her he wanted to get.

Toby didn't doubt scaling her barriers would be hard work, except when he looked at her, with her starched blouse askew and scraped-back hair slightly mussed from their tumble, he couldn't deny he wanted to get beneath her stay-away veneer no matter what it took.

Why he thought there was something worth discovering under Madison's façade, he didn't know. He should take her at face value. Except the saying 'don't judge a book by its cover' kept rolling though his head. And every second he spent with her made him more determined to unearth the real Madison.

MADISON SHIVERED. She wasn't cold. There wasn't a breeze. The early autumn evening was actually quite balmy. No. Her body had gone into some sort of…well, she didn't know what it was doing precisely except she'd never experienced it before.

The only thing that was undisputable was the fact that Tobias Moreland was responsible.

She'd gone all hot and shivery lying in his arms. He was hard. Everywhere. Muscled but not obscenely so, and the hardness in his pants confused her. Did holding her arouse him? The thought had left her fumbling to understand what was happening, and the urge she'd had to rub against him shocked her. Then angered her.

He had no right to make her feel all soft and melty.

And brainless.

Whatever he'd done, it had short-circuited her brain. Even now, several feet away, she could feel the heat radiating off him like the shimmer on a hot summer day rising from a long stretch of black tarmac. It took an extreme amount of control to remain where she was—to not walk up behind him and press herself against his back to soak up all that warmth.

What on earth was that?

"Pull yourself together, Madison," she muttered.

"Huh?" Tobias looked over his shoulder. "Did you say something?"

"Uh, no." She forced a smile. A thin stretch of her lips, no teeth.

He raised an eyebrow in a way that gave her the impression he knew she was lying.

She scrambled for a distraction and hit on what she'd been thinking right before his notable arrival. "You're late." Madison didn't even attempt to keep the censure from her voice.

"Sorry. I was—"

"Don't let it happen tomorrow. We need to leave here at eight. Sharp." She didn't need—or want—excuses. She needed someone she could rely on, who could perform his task on time and properly.

Tobias frowned at her. "Look—"

"No." She pointed her finger at him. "You look. This is an important component in the curriculum for these students. If you aren't able to fulfill your obligation and arrive on time, I need to know now."

The man infuriated her.

She didn't understand the level of irritation he inspired or the rude way she dealt with all these foreign emotions and sensations. Contrary to her recent conduct, she wasn't an ill-mannered person. Or driven to aggravation easily.

Madison knew her current behavior was an overreaction but couldn't seem to stop. She lowered her eyelids and drew in a deep breath. Letting it out slowly, she opened her eyes and focused on the man in front of her.

Had he moved closer?

Striving to keep her voice even and nonthreatening, she said, "Please be on time in the morning. We have to allow for traffic and I don't want to be late for our first guided session."

"I'll be here."

"Yes, but will you be on time?"

He was grinning at her now. Why was he grinning?

"I fail to see the amusement..."

Reaching over, he brushed lose hair away from her forehead. "It's curly."

"What?"

"Your hair." Tobias picked up a strand near her chin. Twirled it around his finger. "It's curly."

"Stop that." Madison slapped his hand away and stepped back as a shiver racked her.

He flustered her. Made her thoughts splinter, shoot off in every direction.

He tipped his head toward the bus. "Anything else need to go in?"

In an effort to clear her thoughts, as well as answer him, she shook her head. "No."

"Right. Let's lock up and grab dinner."

"Dinner?"

"Yes." He slammed the doors and made sure the lock engaged. "You know, food?"

"Oh." Madison shook her head again. "That won't be necessary."

"You don't want to go over the program?"

"No. I have it under control." Madison pushed the alarm button on the bus key.

"Never thought you didn't, but *I* would like to know the details of the excursion before we're there." Tobias gripped her elbow and steered her toward the admin building.

She yanked her arm from his grasp and turned to face him.

"Tobias—"

"Toby."

"What?"

"Everyone calls me Toby. Well, except my mom, but she gets a pass on account of the fact she gave birth to me." He flashed straight white teeth.

Madison was momentarily stunned by his dazzling smile. Shaking her head—*again*—she continued, "Fine. Toby. There's no need to go over the program. Everything is summarized in the file Mr. Richardson gave you. As long as you show up—on time—you'll be doing what's required."

"I'll feel better if you go over it with me. You have to eat, right? So do I. May as well do it together and go over the plan. Kill three birds with one stone. Plus you want me to be prepared for tomorrow, yes?" He gripped her elbow and moved them forward once more.

"Tobias." His fingers tightened, moved across her skin a fraction, and she sucked in a breath as heat traveled up her arm and flooded into her chest like warm caramel syrup.

"Toby." Reaching out, he opened the door and ushered her inside. "And don't bother with another argument. We're getting dinner and going over what you've got planned."

She opened her mouth but snapped it shut when she caught the look he gave her.

He released her. "Go get whatever it is you need from your staffroom. I'll wait here."

"I don't need anything. I packed my car earlier."

"Right. Let's go then."

Opening the door they'd just come through, Tobias propelled her outside with a hand to her lower back. A shudder ricocheted up her spine. Madison wasn't sure if it was frustration, resignation or anticipation. Whatever it was, she didn't have the first clue how to deal with it—or him.

3

TOBY GROUND his teeth and tried to pretend the woman next to him didn't set them on edge. Or get his blood boiling. This morning she'd been waiting for him, arms crossed, one foot tapping the ground, a scowl on her face. A scowl she reserved exclusively for him.

Everyone else got her smiles.

Like now. They sat in a loose circle with their students, discussing the day so far. And she was smiling. Big. Wide. Natural.

Not the forced stretch of lips she occasionally graced him with.

He'd missed a lot of the historic site around them because he'd spent most of his day studying Madison. She was in her element with the students. It was as though she had a split personality—the cold, aloof, sometimes abrasive woman he interacted with and the warm, engaging woman the kids got.

He found himself jealous of a bunch of teenagers.

He wanted this Madison.

It didn't take a genius to work out it came down to comfort

20

and confidence. For some reason, she felt at ease with her students, relaxed enough to let down those walls she hid behind. He'd watched her interact with their guide too, and she seemed as standoffish with him as she was with Toby.

From the corner of his eye, he watched Kim and Rick attempt to sneak off behind their backs and was about to speak when Madison beat him to it.

"Park your behinds back down, you two." She didn't even look at them. "If you're going to attempt to slip away to find a secluded spot to engage in kissing, at least wait until we're all a little more distracted and it's dark."

"*Miss...*" Kim hissed as she flopped down on the grass where they were all enjoying the last of the sun's rays while they ate dinner and waited for their night tour to begin.

"What? You think I don't know you two are dating?" Madison aimed an eyebrow-arched look the young girl's way. "Although I would have thought all the information available on communicable diseases would have turned the two of you off swapping body fluids."

A couple of gasps, a few yucks and even a gagging sound reverberated around the group. Everyone protested Madison's comment in some way except Rick. The kid was grinning for ear to ear.

Toby smiled.

He'd had little to do with these particular students, none of them were in his PDHPE classes or on any of Huntington's sports teams, but he'd found them to be an exceptional group of individuals. He had no clue why they'd been given full-ride scholarships; some no doubt for their genius IQs, others for being classified underprivileged or disadvantaged. What he did know was that each of them took their education seriously, enthusiastically. They were like sponges soaking up every molecule of information.

And they loved Madison Keibler.

The connection between this group of teenagers and Madison was tangible. If he didn't know better, he'd say they'd known her for years. It was a rare teacher who could connect with students that well, never mind that quickly. He'd known she was good at her job. Hard to miss the talk of the 'excellent new teacher' in the staffrooms, hallways and schoolyard, even if he hadn't been hungry for any little detail about her.

He was intrigued before. After spending eleven hours straight with her, not to mention the two hours at dinner last night, he was downright enthralled.

"Sir?"

Snapped out of his thoughts, Toby focused on the boy across from him. "Sorry, Brian. I missed that."

"Do you think we'll see any ghosts?" Brian's voice raised a few octaves with his excitement.

"Um…" He couldn't exactly say he didn't believe in them, could he? "According to all we've been told today and the number of people who've reported seeing one here, I'd think our chances are high."

"I'm sleeping with the light on," Kim said with a visible shudder.

"Don't worry." Rick threw his arm around the girl's shoulders. "I'll sleep in your room to protect you."

"Nice try, Rick." Madison got to her feet. "All right. We've got ten minutes before our night experience guided session starts. Everyone collect your rubbish and dispose of it in the garbage then make a trip to the bathroom. Once we start, we'll be walking around with no pit stops for at least an hour, so if you've got to go, go now."

Toby stood and held open the bag they'd been given to use for their rubbish. Once all the students had dumped their trash and headed towards the toilets, he turned to Madison. "You want to do a bathroom run while I wait here?"

She jolted. "Ah. Sure. Okay."

He smiled. She always seemed surprised when he spoke to her. As though she were ignoring him so well that she completely forgot he was there. He'd like to change that but couldn't do what he really wanted to do to get her attention. Not while they were at work. Unless, unlike Rick, he *did* manage to sneak off somewhere secluded with the woman he wanted to get his hands on.

Then he'd be sure to get Madison's focus solely on him.

Watching her walk away, he marveled at the fact she still looked pristine-fresh. As though she hadn't spent the day wandering around dusty old buildings and along dirt paths. Her hair remained in her usual severe bun, not a strand out of place, and the white blouse with high collar she wore didn't have a crease or sweat mark on it.

The only clue to her day was the dullness of her shoes, their shine reduced by the layer of grime that no one would really notice. Other than that, Madison looked exactly as she had eleven hours ago when he'd first seen her standing by the bus in the school's parking lot.

He wanted to mess her up. Badly. It was like a bindi-eye in his foot. Sharp and stinging until he removed it, but even then the discomfort remained. Toby had a feeling he wouldn't get rid of this particular pain until he'd gotten Madison well and truly ruffled.

ALL DAY MADISON had made a valiant effort to ignore Tobias.

Except he was impossible to overlook.

If wasn't only his size. That alone would need fifty gallons of invisible paint to hide, and last she checked that color wasn't available at the hardware store.

His personality matched his physique in stature and attraction. It was big and friendly and drew everyone in.

The whole Tobias Moreland package was hard to miss.

She'd spent much of the day talking herself *out* of noticing him. When she had to speak to him, she'd been short with her answers and refused to make eye contact, which only served to annoy her further because he was turning her into a rude bitch. And that was something she never thought she'd be.

Her one saving grace had been the students. She'd used them as a buffer.

She was by no means proud of her behavior but it had saved her from having to deal with Tobias for the majority of the time, as well as keeping her mind off the way her body reacted whenever he was near.

The last few hours in particular had proven extremely difficult. He'd seemed to always find her in the dark as they'd been guided around the compound on the hunt for ghosts. Without fail, he'd managed to brush against her as he passed. Stand close behind her, his warm breath drifting over the back of her neck as they listened to their guide explaining the origin of each otherworldly specter believed to be haunting the location they were in.

At one point, he'd even leaned forward and whispered in her ear. Even now Madison had no idea what he'd said. Though she definitely remembered how those whispered words made her feel. She shivered recalling the warm tickle of his breath over her skin, the vibrating hum of his voice in her ear and the flickering hot-and-cold sensation that had swept through her.

Her pulse had pounded and her breathing quickened. And

it wasn't only in those moments when they touched or stood close enough for his heat to sink into her either. She'd been a little out of breath all day. It didn't make sense. Madison didn't even like the man. He was the opposite of everything she'd been brought up to believe.

At least she thought he was.

She had to admit there'd been times during the day when she'd glimpsed a serious side to him, and she couldn't deny he was an attentive and patient teacher with the students. He'd appeared knowledgeable about the history and folklore of the area and not once did she hear him mention any sport. The man was a puzzle, and she feared she might have dealt him an injustice when assuming he was nothing more than a has-been professional sportsman.

She'd heard all about his football career when she'd started at Huntington College.

She sighed. Perhaps that was where her instant dislike had come from. That thought definitely didn't sit well with her.

With a frown, she shook her head and attempted to push all her turbulent thoughts from her mind. She needed to channel some of her earlier resolve and ignore Tobias Moreland's existence. Or she could kiss a good night's sleep goodbye. It would do her well to remember she was at work in spite of the late hour.

Fifteen minutes ago she'd checked the students were in bed with lights out. Hopefully they'd stay there. She didn't foresee any issues, they were a well-behaved group and, other than Rick and Kim trying to sneak off to make out at every opportunity, they'd given her no trouble at all.

She'd agreed with Tobias to take the second shift in the shared bathroom at the end of the hall, and she'd allowed him over an hour to use it and return to his room. Drawing deep breaths and letting them out slowly in an effort to relax, she gathered up her toiletries and headed for the shower.

All was quiet as she made her way along the moonlit hall. They were staying in a six-bedroom cottage. It was one of the original buildings on the grounds and the renovation work done to accommodate overnight stays of school groups had kept with the architecture of the original 1800s building. Each of the rooms had a rustic charm—including the two dorm-like rooms lined with bunks—except the kitchen and bathrooms. Those had all the bells and whistles of modern convenience.

Rounding the doorway into the bathroom, she collided with a hard *bare* chest. The bundle in her arms crashed to the floor on impact and strong arms wrapped around her tightly, forcing her against a wall of heat.

"Whoa." Hot mint-scented breath bathed her face.

Tobias.

Madison closed her eyes. Her heart beat against her rib cage, the thuds reverberating through her torso to settle low in her stomach. They were pressed together from her chest to her knees, and her hands were splayed on the hot stretch of muscle covering his midsection.

"You okay?" His deep voice rumbled through her.

She swallowed. Trembled. "Y-yes."

"Steady on your feet?"

Her legs shook and she leaned into him, her face pressing into his warm chest.

The steel band of his arms tightened. "Madison?"

Her hands flexed, her fingertips inching across his hot flesh, her thumbs moving a fraction lower and encountering the towel wrapped around his hips.

Heat rolled over her. From her curling toes upwards, as though she were slowly sinking into a hot bath; it rose up, tightening and tingling and leaving her breathless.

"Madison?"

He spoke into her hair, the rush of warm breath over her scalp sending a shiver down her spine. The scent of mint and soap and something she couldn't name surrounded her, cocooning her in a bubble of alluring warmth. His muscles rippled beneath her fingers and her mouth watered with the desire to kiss him, lick him—taste every inch of his exposed hot skin.

More unfamiliar urges flooded her. She knew what they were. Knew from an educated position that what she was experiencing was arousal. Sharp and fierce. She'd felt it before, only never this strongly.

Madison tried to catalog each sensation—each emotion—but her reactions were so extreme to any she'd known it was hard to keep track of them. Hard to know what to do with them.

"Madison!" He gave her a little shake. "Are you okay?"

"I..." God what was she doing, plastering herself against him? Feeling him up? She lurched backwards, stepping out of his arms. "Sorry. I didn't see you."

"No worries." She could hear the smile in his voice, if not see it clearly on his face. "I'm finished."

"I'll come back."

"No need." He bent towards her and she jumped back for fear of touching him again. "Let me help you grab your stuff."

Madison stifled a gasp when he dropped at her feet. The moonlight filtering into the hall sparkled off his back, highlighting the undulating muscles in his shoulders, along his spine, as he picked up her toiletries bag and nightgown.

Oh god. He scooped up her underwear.

She held her breath as he slowly rose to his full height. Her eyes felt huge as she stared at Tobias. Before he could say anything—think anything—she snatched her things from his hands and rushed around him into the bathroom. Whirling around, she grabbed the door, all but yelling "thank you" as she slammed it shut between them.

Resting her forehead on the solid timber, Madison barely held off thumping her head against the hard surface. She was such an idiot.

She was *attracted* to Tobias. Intensely.

And he'd had his hands on her underwear!

4

MADISON KEIBLER WAS PREJUDICED.

Toby had never dealt with anyone who had such a narrow-minded view when it came to intelligence. In her eyes, he'd played sport for a living, therefore he was stupid. It was the whole jock-versus-nerd equation on steroids with guns drawn.

He'd been so astounded by her assumptions that he'd been unable to defend himself against her preconceived opinion of his intellect. She'd informed the students to ask her any questions they might have as 'Mr. Moreland doesn't have the level of expertise required to answer'.

Ha!

Wouldn't she be shocked to discover he held more than one degree in education? Personal Development, Health and Physical Education was the one he used for his job as head PDHPE teacher at Huntington College, but he also had bachelors of education in both English and History. He was qualified to answer the students' questions. More than.

He wasn't sure why he'd continued to let her think he was a moron who'd cruised through school and university by the skin of his teeth, but he *did* know when it started to get on his last nerve. Right at the moment he'd realized his attraction to her wasn't minor.

The moment she'd been glued to the front of his practically naked body.

It wasn't that he wanted to impress her with his brain; it was that he wanted her to like *him*—brain *and* brawn—the whole package. He'd worked out Madison didn't tolerate idiots, and she gave him the impression she thought he *was* one, and was enduring his presence only for the benefit of their students. He definitely wanted her to do more than simply *put up* with him.

Toby wanted her to like him so much she wouldn't pull away when he kissed her. From there, he'd convince her to let him do more. For now, he'd settle for that kiss.

A long, hot, wet one.

He grinned. Their little tango in the bathroom doorway last night had been eye-opening. Until that moment, he'd thought the attraction he was feeling went one way. But he hadn't missed the shallow breath, trembling, or the flush that filled her face. And the way she'd snatched her clothes from his hands before slamming the door in his face made him chuckle even now, almost twenty-four hours later.

In spite of her icy attitude that had turned to an artic freeze today, Toby was now one hundred percent sure he was going to pursue Madison. It would be tricky, but she wasn't the first opponent he'd gone up against who appeared unconquerable.

He just needed a game plan. So far subtlety hadn't gotten him anywhere. It was time to rush her defenses.

The last student had just been picked up, and if Toby had to guess, he'd say Madison's turned back and silence meant they were done. Of course, she'd been telling him for the last thirty minutes he could leave. She didn't need him to hang around while the students waited for their rides home.

In what his mother would call 'typical Tobias style', he'd ignored every one of Madison's dismissals.

They'd packed up the equipment and returned the bus keys to the office and unless he could come up with a reason to prolong their time together, Madison would walk away.

He wasn't prepared to let her.

"Don't know about you but I'm starving. Let's grab a pizza and eat while we write up the excursion report." Toby slid his palm under her elbow and steered her towards his car. "We should get it written while the trip is still fresh in our minds."

She yanked her arm from his grasp and spun to face him. "You don't need to contribute to the report. I'll complete it over the weekend and put it in your pigeon-hole first thing Monday. All you need to do is sign and return it. I'll make sure Mr. Richardson receives it."

"You expect me to sign a document without any input?" Toby shook his head. "Oh no. That's not how it works. And if you insist on it, I'll have to fill out my own report to give Ted."

He held her gaze. It surprised him that she didn't back down or look away. Of course, it *shouldn't*. She was tough. Intelligent. Independent. Indomitable. Madison Keibler knew her mind and stood her ground with a stubbornness that tickled some previously unknown need to dominate. To get her to bend.

Toby wasn't a bossy guy by nature. He was the middle brother of five, and if his four brothers hadn't taught him to get what he wanted without pushing others around, their baby sister had. The best life lesson he'd learned from his siblings was patience and stealth.

You didn't need to order people around to get what you wanted. All it took was a little manipulation. He'd convinced more than one brother an idea was theirs over the years. It made for a less confrontational life. Toby had gotten more than enough of that on the football field during his playing days.

"Look. We can do this the hard way or the easy way."

Madison cocked one eyebrow at him.

"You can agree to dinner and doing the report together. Or. You can get in your car and go home."

"I suspect we would disagree on which of those is the easy way."

She was right. He had no doubt she wanted him out of her sight and this whole forced togetherness over with.

Toby grinned. "I should have added what would happen if you choose the 'go home' option."

"Oh?"

"I'd follow."

"Follow?"

He took a step closer, crowded into her personal space. "Follow."

Her throat rolled as she swallowed. "But that's...stalking."

Toby laughed. "It takes a bit more than one colleague following another home to ensure she arrives safely to qualify as stalking."

"Well, yes, but..."

He leaned in. Took a deep breath of her sweet scent. "But...what?"

She licked her lips. Pulled the bottom one between her teeth. "I..."

It was so rare that Madison couldn't put a coherent sentence together but he'd been turning her into a stammering, half-sentence orator for the last two day. Toby felt that right in his gut. He liked that he rattled her enough to stop her brain from ticking.

During their time together, he'd discovered Madison never

stopped thinking. And while an intelligent woman was a turn on, one who overthought was not.

He watched her. Watched the dazed look fade from her gaze and resignation slide in to replace it.

Her shoulders lowered the slightest bit. "Fine. We'll have pizza and fill out the report."

Toby's gut twisted.

He'd gotten what he wanted, only he wasn't happy about it because Madison wasn't happy. Every instinct he had screamed for him to retract. To tell her not to worry—give her an out. Except he knew if he did, he'd never get another shot at being with her outside of school hours.

He grabbed her hand. "C'mon. I know the best pizza place in town."

MADISON ALLOWED Tobias to lead her across the parking lot. His hand was so large it swallowed hers whole. Instead of instilling fear as she thought a man of his size would, he inspired comfort, safety, encouraged compliance.

She didn't understand what had just happened. Oh, she knew she'd agreed to dinner—which would make three nights in a row she'd eaten with him—it was the other thing she couldn't comprehend.

Something had shifted. Some wire had sparked or crossed or broken loose and flapped around, because in those seconds that she'd stared into his dark-chocolate eyes, Madison had wanted to do whatever he asked.

She'd never experienced anything like it.

One instant she couldn't wait to get away from him and the next she had the urge to step forward. Press her body against his and see if he was as hard beneath that polo shirt as he looked...if her memory of his firm muscles rippling beneath her fingers was accurate.

She sighed.

It had taken less than twenty-four hours in his company to work out what it was about Tobias Moreland that rubbed her the wrong way.

He rubbed her the *right* way.

Madison was attracted to Tobias 'Call Me Toby' Moreland.

Her dislike of him wasn't the only thing she'd gotten completely wrong.

She'd labeled him.

Cast him as the dumb jock. Slapped a stereotype cap on his head and dismissed him. And worse yet, she'd insulted him in front of the students by *telling* them he didn't have the expertise to answer their questions.

Could she be any more of a narrow-minded, pretentious bitch?

She owed him an apology.

Except she was afraid that would encourage him to befriend her, and she didn't do friends very well. Not since she'd skipped three grades in high school and been forced to spend time with older peers who found it fun to mess with their socially inept classmate.

"We'll come back for your car." Tobias opened the passenger door of a low-slung sports car.

"Oh, no, I—" She turned her head, tried to move around him.

"Easier this way." He urged her into the seat with one hand at her back and one on her shoulder. "We won't have to search for two parking spots."

She slid into the seat with no further resistance. He shut the door and jogged around the back of the car. Taking a single vehicle made sense. What *didn't* was this meek woman, complying with all his requests.

The driver's door opened. "Look, Tobias—"

"Toby."

"What?"

"Call me Toby. Only my mother calls me Tobias, remember." He buckled his seat belt, started the car and grinned at her. "And it usually means I'm getting an ear-twist in the near future."

"Right. Well, anyway, I don't want to give you the wrong idea—"

He turned towards her, one arm resting along the top of the steering wheel, the other on the back of her seat, and leaned close. "Let's see if I've got the idea so far. You don't want to have dinner with me. You want to go home and write up the report without my input and never have to see me again except in passing in the school halls."

Madison swallowed. "Ah..."

Toby's lips twitched. "I'll take that as agreement."

He wasn't exactly wrong.

"Answer me this. Is it people in general you don't like or just me?"

She sucked in a breath. "I don't know what you mean."

"Yes you do." He moved away, straightened in his seat and put the car in reverse. "We'll table that question for after dinner. Buckle up."

"After dinner?" Madison snapped her belt into place.

He maneuvered the car out of the parking lot and onto the road. "Yeah. I've got plans for our dinner conversation and it doesn't include an uncomfortable Q&A session."

"What does it include?" The fact he'd thought about what they would discuss intrigued Madison.

"Report-filling-out and getting-to-know-you conversation."

"That sounds like a Q&A session to me." She kept her eyes on the road in front of them. Less chance of getting distracted by his strong hands gripping the wheel. His fingers were long and thick, and Madison felt a quiver go through her when she thought about them stroking over her skin.

Toby laughed. "Yes. But it's not the uncomfortable kind. We'll talk about our likes and dislikes, our families and friends, but not the scars left behind by ex-lovers."

"What makes you think—?"

"Madison, you have heartbreak written all over you."

5

"I'VE NEVER HAD my heart broken."

Toby glanced up to find Madison staring at the slice of pizza on her plate. She looked so confused...lost. Which he realized were not regular things for her to be. "What?"

"You said I had heartbreak written all over me, but how can I when I've never had my heart broken?"

Was she kidding? "You've never been in love?"

"I didn't say that."

"So what?" He grinned. "You're the heartbreaker?"

Little creases formed between her eyebrows and he wanted to reach over and smooth them out. "I'm not sure," she murmured.

His grin turned to a frown. "How could you not know if you'd broken a guy's heart?"

Madison sighed and reached for her glass of water—she'd refuse wine. She took a sip before putting it down on the table and finally making eye contact with him.

"I don't think I've ever been *in love*. I've loved. I think. But when we went in different directions it wasn't traumatic or a drama." She chewed the corner of her mouth. "Just...no more."

Toby shook his head. "I don't get it. Did you date idiots?"

"Pardon?"

"Look at you." He waved his hand in her direction. "You're drop-dead gorgeous. You're intelligent. Extremely so. You're independent. I don't see the flaw so it has to be in them."

Color rose up her neck and filled her cheeks with a pretty glow and Toby wondered how far down her chest that wash of blush went. He wanted to peel back the collar of her shirt and find out. He'd nearly had a heart attack this morning when she'd emerged from her room in that top. Gone was the usual shapeless high-necked blouse. In its place was a silky-looking, black, sleeveless button-down shirt that skimmed her collar-bones and revealed an enticing amount of cleavage and had his libido jumping.

He wasn't ashamed to admit he'd tried to catch a glimpse down her top at numerous times throughout the day. Of course he'd had to be ultra-careful, seeing how they were at work and surrounded by twenty very curious, highly intelligent teenagers who were probably more flush with hormones than he was.

Clearing his throat, he tried to yank his thoughts out of her cleavage.

"Thank you."

Her soft words had him leaning forward. It had nothing to do with the fact he wanted to get closer to her. Nothing at all. "Don't thank me for something beyond my control."

"It's polite to thank someone for a compliment." Madison's nose scrunched up, her forehead furrowed, and those lips he wanted to taste curved down on the ends.

"And you're always polite?" He was starting to get a clear picture of who she was. While she'd revealed very little other than she was an only child to older parents—both highly respected in the academic world—she'd given away more by how she said things, her mannerisms.

"Of course."

"Politically correct?"

She nodded. "Yes."

"Not judgmental?"

"No."

"And yet, you labeled me with a stereotype."

Madison's hand stopped halfway to her mouth, her pizza slice held in midair. Her eyes went wide and her mouth parted on a sharp inhalation.

It took her a moment to react, and Toby had to bite his tongue to stop himself from rescuing her from the awkward situation, but she returned the slice to her plate then wiped her hands on her napkin carefully.

She met his gaze head-on. "I'm sorry."

He arched an eyebrow. "For?"

"Judging a book by its cover."

"So I look stupid?"

"What? No!" She frowned.

Toby smiled. "It's okay, I get what you mean."

"No, it's not okay. Not at all." Her frown deepened.

He shrugged. "It's not the first time." Although no other time had bothered him the way it did with Madison. "Probably won't be the last either."

"And that makes me feel worse."

"I don't see how." Toby took a sip of his beer. The only one he was having. Not only was he driving, he needed to have his wits about him for dealing with Madison.

She was quiet for a while and he thought she wasn't going to comment further, but he should have known better than to think Madison wouldn't own up to her prejudice or consider the situation with serious intent.

"I've never done that before. Assumed something about someone I don't know. But with you…"

One delicate shoulder lifted and a pale-pink bra strap slipped from beneath her shirtsleeve to rest on her upper arm. He wanted to peel it all the way down. Right after he undid the six buttons on her shirt—yes, he'd counted them—and pushed it from her shoulders.

"You make me think things I don't normally think." Her skin flushed a rosy pink and her eyelids lowered.

Toby sat up straighter. "Oh?"

"I like you."

He was stunned. She liked him? Grinning, he said, "Jeez. If you think I'm stupid when you like me, I can't imagine what you'd think if you hated me."

It took a moment for that sink in, and when it did, neither of them missed the funny side. Or held back their laughter.

MADISON COULDN'T RECALL ENJOYING an evening more than this one. Couldn't remember ever feeling this comfortable and relaxed—*normal.* She hadn't once second-guessed what to say or felt as though she shouldn't be here. It was a new experience.

After she'd admitted liking Toby—and lord, why had she done that?—they'd settled in to finish their meal and the conversation had flowed between them.

She'd told him things she'd never said out loud before.

Why she'd revealed anything about her lonely childhood was a mystery. All she knew was he made her relax, feel safe. The only time she felt this free was when she dealt with the teenagers she taught.

Their talk hadn't all been a serious rehash of their pasts

either. They'd spoken about books, movies, food, places. In a little less than two hours, they'd crossed several different conversation bridges.

While laughing and talking, they'd eaten their way through a family-size pizza—Toby consuming six slices to her two—and a shared bowl of banana sorbet. Madison popped the last spoonful of the sugary treat into her mouth, closed her eyes and leaned back in her chair with a sigh.

"Damn, that was delicious." She placed a hand on her full stomach.

"Yes. It most certainly is." His voice was a low rumble that vibrated over her skin.

She opened her eyes to find Toby staring at her mouth. Nerves tingled and goose bumps marched down her arms as she slipped her tongue out to lick across her trembling bottom lip. "D-do I have some on my face?"

"No."

"Then—"

"I want to kiss you."

Her stomach flipped. Clenched. "O-okay." The word whispered over her tongue.

"Your mouth. Your neck. Your tits." He leaned in, his eyes darkening with each word he spoke. "Your belly. Your legs. And most of all, I want to press my mouth into the sweet spot I know I'll find between your thighs."

His mouth was centimeters from hers. When had he gotten so close? When had she met him halfway?

Breaths mingled, warm and sweet.

"Tell me I can, Mad." Toby's lips brushed hers. "Tell me I can take everything I want and more."

"Yes." The word hissed through her teeth on a shuddering breath.

Madison thought she knew what to expect. What it would be like to have his mouth pressed against hers.

She was wrong.

So so wrong.

He didn't rush, press hard. There was no demand.

Instead he caressed. Skimmed and shifted until Madison couldn't do anything except chase.

She wanted more than the light, tantalizing brush of his lips.

She wanted the sharp thrust of his tongue.

She wanted deep driving strokes that left her breathless.

The nip of his teeth. Darkly delicious wet heat.

She wanted in a way she never had.

The piercing need that speared through her belly and into her core had her pulling away, jerking back so fast her elbow bumped her glass and sent it flying across the table. Her chair rocked as she sat down hard. When had she lifted out of her seat?

Fingers trembling, she brought them to her mouth.

Toby stared at her. His eyes black, the dark brown obliterated by his swollen pupils. He sucked in haggard breaths, his nostrils flaring wide, and there was a twitch in the line of his jaw that brought to mind strength—control.

"I—" She had no idea what to say.

A determined glint sparked in his eyes. He surged to his feet and pulled his wallet from his pocket. Tossing cash on the table, he growled, "Let's go."

Madison blinked. "Go?"

"Yeah." He shoved his chair out of the way, dragged hers back, and grabbed her hand. Pulling her from her seat, he towed her behind him.

"Where are we going?" Madison asked a little breathlessly. Her short legs worked overtime to keep up with his long ones.

"Home."

"Home?" Her voice squeaked and she sounded like a parrot. Repeating what he said. But her mind was still a little foggy after that kiss.

That barely a *kiss* kiss.

"Yep." Toby pulled open the passenger door of his car and pushed her in. He wasn't gentle, but she couldn't really say he was rough either. More like a ballroom dancer leading his partner around the floor.

He led. She followed.

He slid behind the wheel, the engine roared to life and, with a skill that appeared second nature, he had the sleek sports car zipping out of the car park onto the road before she could think.

6

TOBY SWUNG into his driveway and slammed on the brakes, jolting them forward in their seats.

Madison threw her arm out, palm flat against the dashboard. "Toby!"

"Sorry." He switched off the engine and yanked out the keys. "C'mon."

Keys in hand, he climbed out and headed around to Madison. She'd opened her door and undone her seat belt by the time he got there.

"Toby—"

"Inside." He grabbed her hand and tugged her out of the seat. She was tiny compared to him and it took little effort at all to pull her against him. Wrapping his arms around her waist and lifting her off her feet, he said, "Argue if you want, but do it inside."

She frowned. "How do you know I'm going to argue?"

Toby laughed.

"All right. Fine. I was going to argue."

He couldn't resist dropping a kiss on her pouting mouth. Of

course, one touch and he was at risk of losing control, so he pulled back quickly. "We'll argue inside."

Toby didn't wait another minute to get them behind closed doors. They'd made it through the front door, the lock snapping into place when he slammed it behind them, before he lowered Madison to her feet. He stepped into her, making her take a step back. "I've got a question."

"O-okay." Her back came up against the wall.

"Have you ever done something just because it felt good?"

"Of course."

He shook his head. "No. I mean jumped in with two feet without letting that brain of yours examine it from all angles." Caging her in with his elbows planted on the wall behind her, Toby lowered his head and brushed his cheek over hers. "No thinking. Just feeling."

She sucked in a breath. "I...um..."

"Ever let go." He skimmed his lips up her jaw to her ear. "Ever let a man take you. Ever surrendered to pleasure so complete you felt it all the way to your bones."

Madison trembled and her breathing shortened, growing shallower with every inhalation. "I don't think—"

"Good. That's exactly how I want you."

"W-what?"

"Feeling, not thinking." Toby trailed his tongue along the shell of her ear. Sucked on the lobe. "Feel me, Mad. Feel every inch of me." He pressed his rock-hard cock against her.

"We," her breath caught, "can't."

"Yes we can." He nibbled down her jaw.

She shivered against him. "W-we s-shouldn't."

"Oh yeah." Toby grinned against her silky skin. "We so should."

"But—"

He pressed his mouth to hers. Thrust his tongue between

her parted lips and took them deep. The kiss quickly got out of hand—had both of them groping for purchase.

They had too many clothes on. Toby wanted nothing in his way.

"Naked." He tugged at the buttons on Madison's shirt. "Need to get you naked."

"Wait." Madison's chest rose and fell with her ragged breath. "Stop. I can't think."

"That's the plan, remember?" Toby got her first two buttons undone. "No thinking, just feel... Fuck."

He leaned back, curled his fingers around either side of her top and held the material open. What lay beneath that deceptively innocent shirt...

"Fucking hell. Have you had this on all day?"

"I... What?"

"That bra." Toby couldn't take his eyes off Madison's tits and the delicate pink lace covering them.

She glanced down. "My bra?"

"Yes. That every-man's-wet-dream bra."

"Um...well. Yes. Of course."

"It's a fucking good thing I didn't know before now," he growled.

"It is?"

"Yeah. Because if I'd known you were wearing this under your shirt there's no way I'd have been able to control myself." He went to work on the rest of her buttons. "I want to see you in just the bra."

"Wait. Toby. I don't think—"

"You think too much." He popped the last button free and shoved the shirt off her shoulders. "Help me out here, Mad."

She shook the top from her arms and let it drop to the floor. For someone arguing with her mouth, her actions sure said she was in complete agreement.

"Now the pants."

"Wait." Her hands went to the waistband of her slacks, covering the button and zipper.

Toby laughed. As if that would stop him. To distract her, he palmed her breasts, stroked his thumbs over her nipples through the slightly scratchy lace.

"Oo..."

"You like that?" He increased the pressure of his caresses. "What about this?" He pinched the hardened tips between thumbs and fingers. Gave a little tug to sharpen the sensation.

"Oh god." Madison's head fell back against the wall, her eyelids fluttering closed.

Yeah. She liked that. He gave her nipples another pull. "Mad, we're gonna ditch the pants now."

"Okay." It was more moan than word and Toby grinned.

Before she regained her wits, he popped the button and lowered the zip, then shoved her pants over her hips and down her legs. And just about swallowed his tongue.

Her undies—if you could call them that—matched the bra. Like the bra, the lace was sheer, the sweet curls beneath it playing peek-a-boo and torturing him with the temptation of what the scrap of material barely concealed.

"Fuck, woman. You are so living up to your name." He trailed a finger across the top edge of lace, hip to hip. "Baby, you are going to drive me completely mad if I don't get you out of these now."

Toby didn't wait for Madison to answer, didn't want to hear another argument. He tucked his fingers into either side of her undies and, dropping to his knees, took them to the floor.

The sight before him took his breath. Then again, that could have been her scent. He'd never put too much thought into the way a woman smelled before. Or looked.

But Mad's pussy looked and smelled like the most decadent dessert, and Toby wanted to gorge himself on her.

Leaning forward, he took a deep breath before burying his face between her legs.

MADISON'S BREATH caught in her throat right beside her heart. Toby had his mouth on her. *Down there*. She'd read about it. Heard about it. But she'd never had a guy kiss her like Toby was doing.

He shouldered his way between her legs and the next thing she knew, her thighs were in his hands being pushed up until her feet left the floor. She'd known Toby was strong; she hadn't realized how strong until now. He tossed her around as though she weighed nothing.

Her back was pressed to the wall, her legs draped over Toby's shoulders, and the man's hands and mouth were firmly wedged in her sex. He licked at her. Sucked at her. Stroked and pressed, and everything inside her tightened into a ball of burning need.

She'd had orgasms. Not with a man—but she'd learned her own body and given herself pleasure so she knew what was happening. Except it wasn't like anything she'd experienced. Never had she felt this clawing desperation to reach while feeling the urge to turn back.

This was...was...nothing she ever could have imagined.

Overwhelmed by sensations too intense to grasp on to, she gave in—let them go.

And shattered.

A million brilliant lights flashed through her mind. Electric fire burst inside her, sending every nerve ending into spasms as her climax tore up everything in its path like a category-five cyclone.

She thought she'd called Toby's name. Thought she'd gripped his head to pull him closer—push him away. But when her heavy eyelids lifted, she saw nothing but white.

For a split second she thought she'd gone blind—until she blinked and Toby appeared above her, his face stern. Was he angry?

"Fuck. I have to get inside you."

He fumbled about, and she was on the verge of asking him what was wrong when his body pressed into hers, pinning her harder to the wall at her back, his strong thighs spreading hers. Gripping her knees, he lifted them towards her chest.

"All the way in," he growled against her mouth before thrusting his tongue between her lips.

Madison didn't get a chance to return his kiss. Or breathe. With a brutal shove, Toby drove his body into hers. He stretched her wide. Wider than was comfortable, and she couldn't stop the cry from leaving her throat when pain exploded.

"Shit. Fuck. Mad." Toby cradled her face in his big hands, his thumbs stroking beside her mouth. "Breathe baby. That's it. Take a deep breath for me."

She sucked in air and was surprised to find the pain dissolving into heat—warmth that tingled and spread. "I'm. Okay," she panted.

"No, you're not." He continued to touch her face. Gentle sweeps of his fingers that made her tremble and soften. "Take your time—and while you're doing that, think about why you didn't tell me you were a virgin."

"I...I'm not."

"Mad, you're so fucking tight, there's no way you're not."

She shook her head. "I've had sex." Okay, it was once. Four years ago. But she wasn't a virgin.

Toby frowned. "I don't want to know about anyone who's been here before me. I don't care. What I *do* care about is that I took you like some rutting stud and hurt you."

"It's okay now." She licked her lips, concentrating on the heat and want curling in her pelvis. "It doesn't hurt anymore."

He lowered his forehead to hers. "Dammit, Mad. It's not supposed to hurt at all. Not like that anyway."

Madison could see his intentions in his eyes so she wrapped her arms and legs around him to hold him in place. "Don't pull out."

"Mad," he groaned.

"No. I might not have a lot of experience but I'm not naïve. I know what I want, and that's you. Like this." She rocked her hips against him for emphasis.

"Shit," he hissed, and gripped her hips in his hands. Held her still in a firm hold. "I don't want to hurt you any more than I already have."

"You'll hurt me more if you stop."

Toby grinned. "Baby, I have no intention of stopping. But I can definitely make it better."

7

MADISON COULDN'T STOP herself from cringing as Toby withdrew from her sex. It might not hurt anymore but she was tender—hypersensitive.

"Fuck." Toby's growled curse erupted around them. "C'mon. Let's move this to the bathroom."

"Bathroom?" He'd promised he wouldn't stop. "Toby—"

"Don't panic. We're not stopping." He cradled her in his arms and carried her deeper into the house. "We're just going to do things a little differently."

She couldn't argue with him when she had no real knowledge of what they were doing beyond what she'd learned from textbooks, from the conversations between other women…television and movies. So far, nothing he'd done to her—made her feel—had compared to what she'd known or imagined. "You're the expert."

Toby looked at her with a frown. "Hmm…"

The creases in his forehead drew her fingers and she smoothed them out. "Don't worry. That's a good thing. One of us should know what we're doing."

He didn't look convinced.

Madison opened her mouth to explain further, only to have her words disappear on a gasp. Toby's bathroom was unlike anything she'd ever seen outside of a magazine spread or on one of those beautiful-home type shows on TV.

The far wall was glass; beyond it, a sweeping view of Sydney harbor. It wasn't at all what she would have expected. Not that she'd thought about it, but shouldn't a guy like Toby have black marble and gold fitting and lots of mirrors? In her mind, a bachelor like him would.

That preconceived image certainly wasn't the earth tones, chrome and glass she was seeing. Her gaze scanned every surface. From the floor-to-ceiling glass wall with it's million-dollar view, to the soft caramel-colored tiles in the shower enclosure, to the smooth chocolate-brown tiles beneath his feet, to the dark brown timber counter with a pair of white basins sitting on top.

Calming.

That was the word to describe this decadent space.

Toby walked to the sunken tub and placed Madison on her feet. "Two seconds."

She glanced around. "This is the most beautiful bathroom I've ever seen," she whispered, the space inspiring hushed tones.

He started the water in the tub. "I wanted somewhere I could relax after a grueling game. My brother helped me design the house then oversaw the build."

Her gaze darted to his. "You did this?"

Toby grabbed her hand and tugged her closer. "I didn't build it but the guys who did may as well have plucked the vision out of my head. When I bought the place it was a two-bedroom hovel that needed some serious work." He undid her bra and slipped it from her shoulders; his fingertips grazing over her skin sent a shiver from head to toes.

This man was one surprise after another. "Well, I haven't seen much but it's definitely not a hovel anymore." Madison quivered as Toby ran his hands down her spine and pressed her up against the hard length of his hot naked body. "I—"

"I promise to give you the full tour later. For now…"

She squealed when he picked her up and stepped into the tub.

He chuckled. "Relax. We're going to get to know each other a little better before we get back to what we were doing in the hall."

The reminder sent another shiver through her.

"Cold?" Toby lowered them into the water. "The water will warm you up."

Madison didn't correct him. No point. Besides, he'd positioned her between his legs, her back to his front, his erection pressing into her, and his hands…lord, they were sweeping over her stomach and breasts in long caresses that had her moaning and rocking her hips.

"That's it. Go with it."

She had no idea what he was talking about—or when he'd managed to turn off the water and soap his hands—but thinking became impossible when the man used his big hands and fingers to explore every inch of her.

"You're so soft." He squeezed her breasts. "And hard." He pinched her taut nipples.

Her back arched into his touch. "Toby." She said his name on a gasp. A plea and a protest. For what, she didn't have a clue.

Toby's lips brushed her ear. "You feel so good under my hands. My lips."

His lips trailed the slope of neck to shoulder while those hands travelled lower. He gripped her thighs and raised her legs, pulling them up and over his, opening her wide for his searching touch.

"I'm going to learn all the things that make you tremble. Make you ache." He spoke directly into her ear and made her do exactly that. "Then I'm going to make you come for me again, Mad. Like you did in the hall. You'll do it again and again before I fuck you."

"Oh god." His words sent shards of heat splintering through every cell. Her mind spun but it was her body that spiraled out of control when his fingers found her clitoris.

Toby worked her with speed and skill. In no time, she was panting and begging for more. And he delivered.

"That's it. Take my fingers deeper."

"Please," she hissed as razor-sharp pleasure arrowed through her sex.

"You're still so tight. Sucking at my fingers." He nipped her ear, soothed it with his tongue. "I need you to come now, Mad."

He pressed his thumb on her clitoris, circled, pressed, circled. The fingers buried inside her twisted, stroked and pressed in time with his thumb, and something tripped.

"Toby." His name flew from her lips as the orgasm crashed into her.

She writhed against him but he kept at her, his hand continuing to drive her higher. He slipped his other hand between them. Pushed it beneath her, between the cheeks of her bottom.

Sensation exploded in her pelvis when Toby dragged the tips of his fingers over her anus. Madison's mind fractured. Her body took over, rocking back and forth on both his hands as his fingers probed deeper. There were so many different nerve endings firing to life. Overwhelming her with pleasure—with a hint of pain.

"God, Mad. You are so fucking sexy," Toby growled in her

ear, rocking his erection against her. "I need you to come again, baby. Need it like air."

He increased the pressure on her anus and her clitoris, probed deeper with the fingers buried in her sex. It was too much. Not enough. Right there, ready to drop her into the maelstrom of passion surging like a tidal wave around her.

"Just a little more," he whispered.

Toby drove his fingers into her. Front and back.

Madison went wild. Thrashed and bucked and lost herself in the rush of bliss taking her over.

TOBY COULDN'T WAIT ANY LONGER. She'd taken three fingers with easy and he needed to get his cock in her now or he really *would* go mad.

Grabbing her hips, he lifted her up and got to his knees, sat on his heels. She was small compared to him so spinning her around to straddle his lap didn't take much effort. He hadn't removed the condom he'd put on earlier, and never losing his hard-on kept the protection firmly in place, leaving him with nothing to do but sink inside her tight heat.

He lowered her over him slowly. There was no way he wanted to hurt her again. But she was so fucking tight. Her walls engulfed him. Each millimeter of distance gained left him shaking and sweating and wanting to plunge deep.

She slipped her arms around his neck, buried her face against his throat and moaned her approval as he worked her up and down his shaft. It took all his control to keep the pace slow. The need hurtling through him to take her hard and fast couldn't be satisfied.

Not this time.

Once she was used to him he'd definitely fuck them both into oblivion but for now he'd settle for slow and thorough.

Except Madison had other ideas.

She followed him at first. Then she moved with him. Sitting up, her hands gripping his shoulders, she began riding him with a jerky rhythm that told him more than her tightness that she was inexperienced. But the human body was amazing. Instinct born from centuries of evolution kicked in and Mad rode him as though she'd been doing it all her life.

Toby tried to slow her down by holding her hips, but she used internal muscles to squeeze—to milk his cock in a rolling wave of blinding sensation that had him driving up into her. He'd always been a fan of sex in the bath, but he couldn't recall it ever being this good. This mind-blowing. She was annihilating his self-control with each stroke of her body over his.

"God. Mad. I'm close." He panted. "Come with me."

It wasn't a request. He wouldn't go over without her. He reached for her breast, pinched a nipple, twisted and tugged, before moving lower to the hard knot of nerves at the top of her pussy.

She bucked in his arms.

"Oh yeah." Toby stroked in time with his thrusts. "C'mon, Mad. Come all over my cock."

Her hips picked up speed, the rock and roll driving her up and down his cock and into his hand at a frenzied pace that had them both gasping for breath and moaning with pleasure. He leaned forward. Slanted his mouth across hers and thrust his tongue between her lips.

The kiss was aggressive. Desperate. They were on the cusp of release and neither of them seemed willing to go over first.

"C'mon." Toby pushed up harder. Faster. Pulled her down with his arm around her back.

She whimpered. "Toby."

"I know."

They slammed together in a furious rush that sent water splashing over the side of the tub.

"I feel it, Mad. It's right there." He pounded into her harder. "Let me have it."

She constricted around him, her orgasm finally breaking. Her pussy squeezed his cock until he had no choice but to follow her over.

He came hard. Ground her down against him and emptied what felt like his soul inside her.

8

MADISON COULDN'T BREATHE—COULDN'T move.

Definitely couldn't think.

She tried to get something to connect. A thought. A word. Anything that wasn't washed in the delirium of satisfaction that swamped her.

Toby's hold tightened. "You still with me?"

She managed a nod. Half a grunt.

He chuckled. "Yeah. Definitely that good."

Letting her head roll to the side, she forced her eyes open and gazed at him. His eyes were hooded, their dark brown depths swimming with so many emotions. Satisfaction, triumph, pleasure, lust. The way he stared at her had her pulse skipping, heat rising—her body tightening.

His mouth tipped up on one end. "Ready for round two?" He rocked up, his shaft hard inside her.

Her eyes popped wide and her head snapped up from his shoulder. "Didn't you—"

"Absolutely did. But I'm not done with you." He surged to

his feet; water rushed around the tub, over the side, and, stepping out, he took her with him.

"Toby," she squeaked and held on.

Grinning, he said, "Change of scenery."

He walked them into the bedroom, the one she'd missed on their earlier trek to the bathroom. Wasting no time, he got her on the bed, his body pinning her to the mattress, his hard penis still buried deep. How he accomplished that feat was a mystery.

"Need to change condoms."

Madison gasped when he pulled out. Over-sensitized tissues protested, clutched at his retreating flesh with greedy contractions.

Toby smiled wide. "Don't panic. I'll be right back."

She had no doubt he would be.

But other doubts began to creep in. What was she supposed to do now? Was there some form of etiquette for this kind of encounter? Should she slip under the covers or remain on top?

"Why the frown? Are you in pain?" Toby strolled into the room completely unconcerned by his nudity.

And why wouldn't he be confident? He was gorgeous. It was more than evident he looked after himself.

"Mad?"

Oh, right. "No. I'm not in pain. A little discomfort, that's all." She clamped her legs together and folded her arms across her torso.

He arched one eyebrow. "Any reason you feel the need to hide?"

"I..." Madison tried to swallow the ball of nerves in her throat. "I don't know what to do."

"About?" He tossed a row of foil packets on the side table

and climbed on the bed, stretching out beside her. But he didn't touch her.

She had no reference for this type of thing. The one time she'd had sex, the guy had been gone within minutes of ejaculation. He hadn't even taken his pants off all the way so it was a quick removal of protection and zip up before heading out the door. She regretted allowing that relationship to go as far as intercourse. She'd been thinking of ending things and ended up losing her virginity.

One of many signs she wasn't good at interacting with others.

"You're having some sort of internal struggle." Toby tapped her temple with a fingertip. "I can hear your mind spinning."

"Well, yes, there's a lot to think about."

"Why?"

"Um..." Madison hated being unable to pull her thoughts together and around Toby it appeared to be her go-to mode. She latched onto the obvious. "We're naked, for one."

Toby laughed. "And we're going to stay that way the rest of the night."

"Rest of the night?"

"Yep." He nodded. "I told you I wasn't done."

"Ah, yes, you did, but—"

His hand covered her mouth. "Stop thinking. Remember how well it turned out last time you switched off that brain of yours?"

She spoke against his palm. "We had sex." Great sex. The greatest-sex-in-the-world sex. Her world, anyway. His...

"Amazing sex," he growled as he replaced his hand with his mouth.

Madison parted her lips for his probing tongue. She shivered when he trailed a hand down her chest and over her breast to the taut nipple that throbbed and tingled, anticipating his touch. He didn't disappoint. His fingers played—stroked, pinched and twisted—until her breath puffed from her lungs in shallow pants.

"I can't get enough of you," he spoke into her mouth, the words low and muffled. "The need shouldn't get stronger."

With trembling fingers, Madison touch Toby's broad chest. His moan of pleasure rippled through her and made her bolder. Tentatively she explored his torso, the wide pecs and the undulations of his abdomen. She'd never seriously thought about the references other women made to washboard abs, but having Toby's warm muscles beneath her hand brought new understanding.

He continued to kiss her. His tongue tangled with hers and explored her mouth with wet slides that coaxed her to do her own explorations. More confident, she thrust her tongue against his and moved her hand lower on his body, investigated those sharp dips that ran along his hipbones and led to his groin. Proving he was in tune with her, Toby pulled his mouth from hers and rolled to his back.

"Touch me wherever—however—you want." He raised his arms and folded them beneath his head. "I'm all yours."

"Oh." Her eyes widened as she took in all of him. From head to toe, the man was sculpted perfection. Smooth skin stretched over muscles honed to peak condition. Light brown hair, sparse in some places, thick in others, had her wondering if it would feel coarse or soft against her fingertips—her face. "I've never..."

"Just what have you done?" His last word hitched when she trailed her fingertips down his stomach towards the large erection protruding from his groin.

"I've had sex." The deep channels edging his abdominal muscles intrigued her. They formed a natural arrow toward what was surely the world's most magnificent penis. She wrapped her fingers around his thick shaft.

"Fuck." He jerked in her hand, his hips rising off the bed, and she instantly let go.

"Sorry."

"No." He grabbed her hand and moved it back to his penis. "That was a good fuck."

With his guidance, Madison gripped him once more and began to stroke up and down his length. "It's so smooth." There was no hiding the wonder in her voice.

"Have you ever touched a cock before?" His words were tinged with curiosity and disbelief.

She shivered at the earthy description of the flesh in her hand and, shaking her head, she continued to examine the silky skin stretched wide and long, as well as the crinkly skin covering the testicles at the base. "It's completely different to what I expected."

TOBY'S HEAD was going to explode.

Both of them.

"Yeah. Like that." He rocked up into Madison's hand.

She'd gripped him with uncertainty at first, now she worked her hand over his cock with the confidence of someone who knew her touch brought pleasure. He pulsed in her palm and she squeezed her fingers tighter, more blood rushed into his shaft, making him harder.

God. He threw his head back on the pillow and grit his teeth. Had a hand job ever felt this good?

She learned quickly what set him off. The sweep of her thumb over his crown on the upstroke, the roll of his balls on the down, and the slight twist of her wrist with every pull.

She'd mastered him without even trying. Her innocence and curiosity added to the pleasure.

He'd figured out Madison had limited sexual experience and he was willing to let her explore to her heart's content. He just wasn't sure he could handle it without giving her a handful. And he wasn't talking about his junk currently in her hand. If she kept it up, he'd be dumping a load all over both of them.

"Can I make you ejaculate?"

Fuck. His body went rigid, his groin throbbed. Even her clinical words got him off. "You want to give me a hand job?" he rasped out through clenched teeth.

"Is that okay?"

Toby laughed then groaned when her fingers tightened around him. "Fuck. Yes. Whatever you want." He'd stand on his fucking head and suck his damn thumb if she kept doing what she was doing.

"When you do, can I taste it?"

Jesus. Shit. Fuck. He pumped his hips, drove his cock through her tight grasp. "Harder. Faster."

"Like this?"

"Argh..."

"And this?" She cupped his balls in her other hand, squeezed gently, rolled them. "Does that feel okay?"

"Yes. Everything." He panted. "Don't. Stop."

Fuck. He was ridiculously close to coming. Embarrassingly close.

Her grip grew tighter and quicker and Toby's eyes crossed as she took him over the edge. Hips bucking, his cock jerked with each pulse of come spilling from the head. Sperm coated his belly and Madison's hand, the glide of her fingers easier with the aid of his natural lube.

"Jesus. Mad." He dragged in a breath and clamped his jaw

as she lowered her head and tentatively licked at him. "Fuu...ck."

She took him into her mouth, her lips stretching around the crown and sliding down his shaft a good couple of inches. A hum vibrated through him and settled in his balls. They may have just emptied a load but he'd be damned if they weren't tingling and throbbing like they were ready to launch another one.

She increased the suction as she lifted off him. "It's salty." She took a swipe at the pool of come on his stomach with the flat of her tongue. "Not as creamy as I expected."

Every part of him went rock hard. Include the cock that had just exploded in release.

Jesus, she was killing him. Her guileless commentary of her discoveries, the way she studied his come with an innocent fascination, shouldn't turn him on. It did. Everything about her captivated him, from her prudish schoolmarm persona, to this curious sexually uninhibited woman lapping at his cock—and the many facets of Madison in between—Toby wanted to know them all.

He wanted to be the one to show her new things. Watch while she explored a world of pleasure she'd either been denied or denied herself. Whatever the reason, he planned to be the one to show her everything she'd missed.

Starting with one of his favorite positions.

Gripping her waist, Toby spun her around and brought her over the top of him so she faced his feet. "Put your knees on either side of my head," he demanded.

She did so without question and he smiled. Wiggling a bit, he lined himself up so his face was right near that sweet pussy of hers.

"How do you feel about math?"

"What?" She arched her back and tucked her head, staring

at him through the gap between their torsos. "I don't understand."

"I'm gonna teach you all about the number sixty-nine." He rocked his hips so his cock brushed the side of her face. "Suck me while I lick you."

Her eyes widened, a harsh breath rushing through her parted lips as she turned and brought her mouth a millimeter from his throbbing length. "Mmm..."

Toby didn't need to say anything else. Not that he could. The second she parted those plush lips and sucked him inside, he wasn't capable of making anything with his vocal cords other than animalistic sounds of pleasure.

Lust whipped at him. Clawed and dragged as ecstasy lashed through him. Wanting nothing more than to take her with him—to make her feel the deep erotic thrill that rocked him to his bones—he leaned up and all but swallowed her slick pussy whole.

In minutes they were dancing on the brink of release. Moving together faster and faster until Toby couldn't hold out any longer. His third orgasm of the night tore through him as though it were the first. It took him hard and without mercy.

He barely registered the tight suction of Mad's mouth as she drew every drop of come from him. Heart racing, breath heaving in his chest, he used his fingers and thumb to shove her off the cliff with him.

She cried out around his cock and another spasm gripped him. Groaning against her thigh, he gentled his strokes, eased her down as the last of her release rippled through her.

Sapped of energy, it took effort to spin her so she lay draped over his chest, her head snuggled beneath his chin. He wrapped his arms around her and held her close. Her ragged breath and heart beat lulling him to sleep.

9

"MORNING." Toby nuzzled his nose on the soft skin in the curve of Madison's neck.

She turned into him, snuggled against his chest. "Hmm... what time is it?"

Her sleepy voice purred over him, making him smile. He could get used to waking up to her. Glancing at the clock, he said, "Barely nine."

"God." She groaned. "We haven't even had four hours' sleep."

He smiled. "Yeah, but the day's a-wastin'." Toby slapped her ass and rolled out of bed. "We've got plans."

"Plans?" Her tussled head came off the pillow and she aimed wide, sleepy eyes his way. "We don't have plans."

"We most certainly do. Starting with a shower." He scooped her up in his arms—something he was becoming fond of doing—and carried her to the bathroom.

"Tobias."

Her indignant cry made him grin. "Madison."

"Put me down."

"Sure." Walking into the shower, he lowered her to her feet. "Happy now?"

She scowled up at him, opened her mouth, but whatever she was going to say turned into a shriek when he flicked on the tap and a burst of cold water hit them.

Laughing, Toby wrapped an arm around her waist and spun her around so her back was to the wall. "Let's make sure you're good and dirty before we clean you up."

"Toby..." She gasped and shivered as he ran his tongue down her throat on the way to his knees.

He'd discovered last night Madison found particular pleasure in having his mouth on her. Wrapping his hands around her thighs, he lifted her up and brought her legs over his shoulders. Pink flesh, already glistening with her arousal, spread before him. He leaned in and feasted.

She gripped his head, twisted her fingers in his hair and rocked her hips toward him. He took her up fast. Pushed her to the razor's edge of release and held her there until she begged.

"Please." She tugged on his hair. Thrust her pussy against his mouth. "More."

He gave it to her. Teeth and tongue and lips. Fingers plunging hard and deep, and the pressure of his thumb on that tight rosette he'd yet to fuck. They'd get to that. Not today though. Today he was going to make her come, and while she was all soft and compliant, he'd get her to agree to join him at his family's barbeque.

With his goal in mind, Toby sucked her clit between his lips and flicked with his tongue as he drove three fingers into her clenching pussy. She jerked. If it weren't for the wall behind her, supporting her back, they would have toppled to the floor.

Her orgasm broke over her and she writhed against him.

His fingers sank deeper with each contraction and the thumb pressed to her anus breached that virgin territory.

A cry tore from her throat. The extra stimulation set off a new wave of spasms and Madison became a livewire in his arms. She thrashed and bucked and dug her nails into his scalp. He rode it with her, kept up the carnal assault until the final quake turned to a tremor. And still he kept at her, brought her down from that high peak to the melted valley of release.

She went limp, her body draping over his head and, slipping her legs from his shoulders he settled her onto his lap, her thighs straddling his. He stroked a hand over her hair—still in a bun but now thoroughly messed and hanging from the back of her head with all they'd done in the last twelve hours—down her back and waited for her breathing to return to normal.

"You okay?" he murmured into her temple where he nuzzled the wisps of wet hair.

"Mmm..."

Toby smiled and held her close. He'd known beneath Madison's cool exterior he'd find layers, but he never dreamed he'd find the responsive woman currently in his arms. Time and again during the night she'd proven to be his equal in sexual appetite, and her willingness to try anything he suggested blew him away. Her proclivities appeared to be a match for his as well.

She stirred in his arms and he was reminded again of her size. At least a foot shorter than him with delicate bones that disguised surprising strength, Madison was a deceptive package. She'd handled him with ease, even when she'd been unsure of herself she hadn't backed away; she'd gone after what she wanted.

What *he* wanted was to know every inch of her. Inside and out.

And he didn't just mean physically.

He wanted to know what made her tick. What she liked and didn't. Where did she see herself in five years...ten? Did she want to get married? Have children? Continue to teach or stay at home to raise her family? So many questions. But he wouldn't find the answers sitting at the bottom of his shower.

"Up we get." He got to his feet, held her pressed against his chest and turned under the water. "Good thing I've got instant hot water."

Madison tilted her head back to look at him with a contented smile. "Good thing."

He returned her smile with a wide one of his own. "Let's use it to get you clean, now I've made you all dirty." He spun her around, put her on her feet, and reached for the soap with one hand while keeping the other curled around her waist. "Stand right there."

When she was steady, he lathered his hands and proceeded to turn a simple wash into a sensual massage. When her head lowered, her chin hitting her chest, he made his move.

"Want to get some breakfast here or on the way to your house?"

"I can make French toast if you have the right ingredients."

Toby grinned. "Excellent." He ran a hand up her spine, getting a moan as reward.

"Do you have coffee?"

"Who doesn't have coffee?" Dragging both hands up her ribs, he moved them around to cup her tits. "We need to go to the shops to pick up some steaks for later."

"Okay." She moved into his touch, her back arching, her boobs lifting into his palms.

"We'll stop at your place on the way so you can get changed."

"Mmm... Okay." Madison languidly leaned back against him.

He dropped a kiss on the top of her head and gave her tits one last squeeze before turning her under the spray to wash away the remaining suds.

MADISON'S GAZE flicked to the rearview mirror and the man following her. She was more than a little befuddled at what was going on. So much had changed since Wednesday when she was forced to accept Toby as her co-teacher.

They'd spent the night together.

Technically they'd spent two nights together, but last night had been nothing like the first one. The things he'd done to her —with her. The things she'd done to *him*. Even now, a flush rose up her chest and heated her face. Her sex clenched, her nipples pebbled. From her tumbled hair to her rosy cheeks to her sore muscles and intimate parts, her whole body was one big blooming advertisement for lascivious activity.

She looked like she'd spent the night rolling around in bed having hot sex. The look was so foreign, Madison kept doing a double take whenever she caught a glimpse of herself. And she didn't even want to think about the roller coaster of emotions or the barrage of sensations swamping her.

A part of her wanted to just go with it. Wanted to let him lead her wherever he chose to take them. She'd been doing that since last night and so far he'd given her amazing pleasure and made her feel sexy, desired—normal. He was the first man to ever make her feel those things.

She'd spent her whole life a step apart. Not by choice. Circumstances had led her to the fringes of whatever environment she was in. From the age of thirteen she'd been surrounded by people older than her. Not that she'd ever really interacted with those her own age before that. Her parents had her on a strict study regime that didn't allow for socializing with other kids.

There was no frame of reference for her interaction with Toby. She didn't know what to think or what to do or how to act.

She'd never felt so out of control.

He overwhelmed her. Took her to places she'd never dreamed of and had her wanting more—craving more.

Which is where the other part of her came in. She didn't understand why a man like Toby would want *her*. Sex aside, which she was smart enough to know any guy would take, no matter who offered, why did he want to be with her?

With a sigh, she flicked her indicator on and prepared to turn onto her street. Another quick glance in the mirror showed Toby right behind her.

The idea of spending the rest of the day with him sent a thrill through her. Excitement with a twinge of fear zipped along her nerves and buzzed in her ears. The urge to smile *and* frown as her mind fought over whether to be happy or not about the coming hours confused her more.

How could she have two conflicting emotions about the same thing?

It was times like these—not that she'd had them all that often—that she wished she had a best friend. Or any friend. She'd lived almost twenty-seven years without any real friendships. She had acquaintances, during school and later at work, but no one close enough to share things with, confide in. The two men she'd dated in her early twenties didn't count. One lasted a total of four dates and the other four months.

Neither had left a lasting impression. Even giving her virginity to Gerard hadn't made an indent. She hadn't valued that as a prize or a precious gift and now she wondered why. Shouldn't something like that be special? Something she could look back on with fond memories or at least some sort of emotion other than indifference?

Would Toby have valued that privilege?

Pulling into the driveway of her modest clapboard house, she shook her head and concentrated on now. There was no point rehashing things she couldn't change. She hadn't understood why she'd let things go so far at the time, rewinding the incident now wouldn't bring her clarification.

A tap on her window made her jump. Turning, she found Toby beside her car smiling in a way that had her own lips tipping up.

Madison might not understand what was happening between them but she knew she didn't want to miss a second of it. For the first time in her life she felt involved—alive. It was a strange feeling. Not anything like the pleasure she got from teaching, which up until now had been her only source of enjoyment.

Her door opened and Toby offered his hand. Smiling wider, she placed her hand in his and let him pull her from her seat. She laughed when he tugged her against him and dipped her over his arm.

"What are you doing?" She sounded breathless and her pulse sped up.

He grinned. "I missed you," he said before dropping his head and planting his mouth on hers.

Her lips parted under the pressure of his and when he swept his tongue into her mouth, she stroked it with her own. He may have started the kiss and she might not have had that much experience with the sensual act before meeting him, but she was a damn fast learner. And contrary to her initial beliefs about Toby, he was a damn good teacher.

He broke their lip lock and righted her. "C'mon. Let's go. We'll be late if we don't hustle."

"What are we doing again?" She led the way to her front door.

"The shops to grab some food, then to a barbeque."

Madison glanced over her shoulder. "With...?"

He smiled and brushed a fingertip down her cheek. Tapped her chin. "It'll be fine. You'll be fine."

How did he know she was worried? The man appeared to have either mindreading powers or her forehead had acquired an LED screen that flashed her thoughts.

Pulling her into his arms, he dropped a kiss on her nose. "I promise. I won't leave your side. You've got nothing to be scared of."

Easy for him to say. He'd probably never been in a situation where he felt out of place or totally inept. Those two things pretty much summed up every interaction she'd had from the time she'd graduated high school at thirteen.

Stretching her lips into a wobbly smile, she said, "All right. What's the dress code for this barbeque?"

The last thing she wanted to do was look out of place before she even opened her mouth. Of course, once she did, everyone would know she was socially clueless.

"You got any sexy summer dresses?"

Madison glanced at the overcast sky. "It's not exactly warm enough for that."

"Hmm...okay, as long as it's not one of those skirt-and-blouse combinations you wear to work, I'm sure whatever you think is good for a casual backyard barbeque will be fine."

Great. No help at all. She'd never been to a backyard barbeque. She unlocked the front door and walked inside, Toby right behind her, contemplating what she had that would fit in with the type of event he described.

She remembered the lovely pantsuit she'd bought on a

whim last year and never worn. It had a halter-neck top but she could throw on one of her light cardigans for warmth.

Heading down the hall, she called over her shoulder, "Back in a minute. Help yourself to a drink if you want."

"Sure you don't want any help?" Toby yelled after her.

Laughing, she said, "What, like you *helped* me in the shower?"

The grumbling moan that followed her into her room sent a thrill through her middle to pulse in her sex.

Need stirred. Lord. For someone who'd had more sex in the last twelve hours than she'd had in her whole entire life, she was craving more.

Toby had her stepping out of her comfort zone with every second they spent together. And while the thought brought fear, Madison felt excitement and joy at the prospect of spending even more time with him.

10

TOBY GRIPPED MADISON'S hand tightly. She was half a step behind him and he had to tug on her arm a little to get her to keep up. Not that he was walking too fast for her. It was her sudden reluctance to be here that caused her to drag her feet.

"It'll be fine." He gave her hand a gentle squeeze.

"I don't think…"

He stopped and pulled her into his arms. "You're not thinking, remember."

"But—"

He pressed his lips to hers and spoke against them. "What do you want to do? Don't think about what the *right* thing is. Ignore the fear. Do you *want* to spend the afternoon with me?"

"Yes."

Toby grinned, popped a quick, hard kiss on her then pulled away. "See? You should definitely be here."

"But it's a family thing," Mad argued.

"You'll soon see the Morelands have a different view on what makes family."

She opened her mouth but before she could get a word out,

he spun around and tugged her through the side gate to his parents' backyard.

At a glance, it looked as though they were the last to arrive. Smiling, he pulled Mad under his arm and walked into the middle of his sister and sister-in-law's combined baby shower.

Cassie and Shaye held court, side by side, in two expertly carved rocking chairs he knew his Gramps had made. The man might be pushing eight-six but he could still work magic with wood. He had no doubt Granny had made the soft-looking baby blankets both women had in their laps.

Making a beeline for the stars of the day, Toby smiled and nodded as he maneuvered them toward his targets.

"Toby!" Cassie jumped to her feet and threw her hands on her hips. "You're late."

He grinned. "Better me than you. How long now? Five days?"

"Five, forever, same dif." Cassie's eyes rolled then widened when she caught sight of Madison beside him. She arched on delicate eyebrow. "Did you bring me a present?"

Chuckling at her, he said, "Not yet." He glanced at Shaye. "Coop's got that covered this year. Hey, Shaye."

It was a running joke in their family that Cassie wanted a sister for her birthday every year, and when he'd asked about a present for the baby, she'd told him the baby wanted an aunty.

Looking around, he tried to find his youngest brother. "Where's Zac? Didn't he get you what you want too?"

His sister ignored his question and held out her hand to Madison. "Hi, I'm Cassie, Toby's sister."

"Oh." Mad's cheeks flushed as she untangled herself from his grip. "Sorry. Hi. Madison."

"Sorry. Mad, the other glowing lady is my sister-in-law, Shaye."

"Hi." Shaye waved.

"Nice to meet you." Madison smiled a little nervously and Toby gave her hand an encouraging squeeze.

"Toby, get Madison a chair." Cassie waved at the area beside her rocker. "She can sit with us."

Madison's fingers trembled in his. "I...um..."

He pulled her back against him and aimed a glare at Cassie. "I'm going to introduce her around before you start any inquisition."

Cassie exaggerated a pout as she sat back down. "Fine. Ruin all my fun."

"Cassie." The warning came for Cassie's husband, Luc, as he stepped up behind her chair. "You'll have to excuse my wife. She's a little grumpy today."

"What do you expect? I'm not allowed to breathe without prior consent. I'm bigger than a whale, I have to pee every three minutes and I haven't seen my toes in weeks."

"Oh god. Is this what I have to look forward to?" Shaye asked.

"And those are the highlights, don't get me started about peeing your pants when you sneeze," Cassie growled.

"Cass." Luc placed his hand on her shoulder and Toby watched as his sister visibly relaxed, all but melting under his touch.

It still amazed him that anyone could control the hellion that was Cassie. He supposed growing up with five older brothers had something to do with the fact his baby sister took no shit and dished it whenever the chance arose.

"Speaking of peeing..." Cassie pushed to her feet again.

"Wooee...hot damn, now the party's getting started. Who's this sexy creature and where have you been hiding all my life, gorgeous?"

"Gramps!" Cassie gasped.

"What?" Gramps didn't take his eye off Madison and Toby

smiled and slipped his arm around her shoulders in reassurance.

"You can't say stuff like that," his sister reprimanded.

"Why the hell not? I've got eyes. She's a pretty little thing."

"That may be but she doesn't need a dirty old man telling her that," Cassie argued.

"Humph." Gramps crossed his arms over his barrel chest. Unlike most elderly, Gramps hadn't hunched or lost his robust form with age. "I'd rather be a dirty one than a dead one."

Luc hid a chuckle behind his beer.

"And what's wrong with telling a pretty woman she's a knockout?" Gramps asked.

"Well..." Toby rubbed his chin while pulling Mad more snuggly against his side. "It might have a little to do with the delivery. The whole undressing her with your eyes and leaning in with your tongue hanging out was a bit much, old man."

Gramps pointed a slightly crooked finger at him. "And that right there is why. I'm *old*. I don't got time to waste on tact."

Toby laughed. "Where's Granny?"

"Shit!" Gramps spun around, a full three-sixty. "Jeez. Give an old man a heart attack why don'tcha." He thumped his hand on his chest for emphasis.

"There's no chance of that. You're too stubborn to have a weak heart." Cassie grabbed Gramps's elbow. "Now walk me inside to the bathroom. This great-grandchild of yours is playing punch-the-bladder again."

"Now, Princess, I told you we should get one of them porta-loo thingies so you didn't have to keep going inside."

"I'm not peeing in a plastic box in my parents' backyard!"

Gramps patted Cassie's hand as they moved away. Before they were out of earshot, he fired a look over his shoulder at Toby. "And don't think for one second I'm not coming right back to you to find out how you managed to punch so far above your weight, young man."

Toby shook his head. "I swear, he's getting worse with age."

"He's always been a rascal." Granny stepped in front of Toby. "How are you, my favorite grandson?"

"Aw, Granny, you say that to all your grandsons." Toby leaned down and placed a kiss on his grandmother's cheek.

"Besides, everyone knows I'm her favorite." Toby's oldest brother, Damian, joined the conversation. "And I *was* first."

"By one day," Toby argued. "Mum beat Aunt Janet by one day."

"Still first." Damian raised his beer bottle.

Ignoring him, Toby turned back to Granny. "Mad, this is my grandmother, Margaret. Granny, meet Madison."

MADISON ENDEAVORED to keep everyone's name straight but there were so many people. Usually putting names to faces wasn't an issue except this wasn't the normal teacher/student interaction. She'd taken part in little conversation because she didn't know what to say or how to contribute most of the time.

She was so used to offering information on a subject and then answering questions or discussing the topic of choice that entering into normal, everyday conversation was proving beyond her.

And everyone here had such a rich history together. They were all so relaxed and comfortable with each other. Madison couldn't help but feel envious of their connections and ease. These people—this family—were everything hers wasn't.

The out-of-control feeling she'd had earlier had multiplied by one thousand. It threw her back to those horrible years of school where she'd sat on the fringe of her peers and watched them interact with confidence, leaving her with a sense of inadequacy and loneliness. All those quiet times spent in libraries, in her room, studying, her only connection to the world the words on the pages in front of her.

Always a part of something and yet not...

Hollowness filled her. Sadness.

"Hey. You okay?" Toby wrapped an arm around her shoulders.

She turned her head and forced a smile. "Yes."

The last thing she wanted was for him to know how uncomfortable she felt around his family. He'd introduced her to everyone over the course of the afternoon and while she'd attempted to talk to all of them, she just didn't have the skills to go deeper than the most superficial conversation. Her efforts barely scratched the surface of 'nice weather we're having'.

"Are you sure?"

His concern warmed her. Turned her smile genuine. "Yes. Just a little tired. Overwhelmed."

"Yeah, this lot can be a bit much to take even when you're used to them. Why don't we cut out? We can go home and watch a movie."

"Oh, no." She didn't want to make him leave his sister and sister-in-law's combined baby shower. It was bad enough that she felt like a gatecrasher. "You should stay. I'll call a cab."

"What?"

The more she thought about that idea, the better it sounded. She needed some time alone to process everything and she really was tired. "You can stay and enjoy the rest of the party and I'll see you Monday at work."

Reminding herself that they were coworkers only increased her urge to flee.

"I'll just say goodbye to Cassie and Shaye." Madison pushed to her feet. "Thank your parents for having me here."

Toby stood. "Let's go."

"No. No. You don't have to come with me."

He gripped her chin lightly but firmly, making it impossible to avoid his gaze. "You're here with me. You leave. I leave."

"But—"

"Don't argue, Mad. You won't win." Toby wove his fingers through hers and tugged her toward his sister and sister-in-law.

"Toby."

"Not another word other than goodbye to my family, Madison."

Well, there was no denying the hard edge of his voice. Neither could she ignore the little tremor that ran through her at his commanding tone. He'd used that voice on her in bed and she shivered with remembered sensation. What was it about this man ordering her around that heated her blood and softened her muscles? She yielded to his demands and did it willingly.

She'd never been malleable. Never let anyone, other than her parents, tell her what to do. Somehow Toby controlled her. Did it in a way she not only accepted but welcomed.

What on earth had he done to her?

He'd gone from someone she barely tolerated to someone she wanted to spend all her time with. And it wasn't only his bedroom skills that appealed to her.

She'd discovered so much about the man today.

He loved his family unconditionally. Even those who weren't blood related got the same level of consideration, the same genuine interest and respect from Toby. He freely showed his affection too. With his family. With her. It wasn't something she was used to and it took her by surprise every time he directed his attention towards her.

But she was beginning to crave that part of him. Wanted to

be on the receiving end of one of his infectious smiles or his care and concern for her wellbeing.

Madison hadn't felt that level of interest ever. Not even her parents were as attentive to her welfare beyond the rudimentary necessities of raising a child. Unlike the family surrounding her, with its warmth and love, her parents had made sure she was fed and clothed but done little in regard to emotional nurturing.

If she were honest, she'd never felt loved by her parents. She'd just assumed they held that sentiment in regard to her. After spending the afternoon with the Morelands she doubted her parents even knew what real love was. *She* didn't understand the depth of emotion this family showed one another. Not with any true knowledge.

She grasped the concept in an intellectual capacity but when it came to the sentiment itself Madison had no personal exposure to drawn on. What she felt for her parents didn't compare to what she'd witnessed exchanged between Toby and his family. Or even between her and Toby.

Madison wasn't sure she was capable of such a profound connection though. Surely she would have encountered it by now if she were? Was what she was experiencing with Toby the beginning of a deeper relationship?

So much to think about. Too much to explore while in the presence of the man himself. He'd already proven he short-circuited her brain. She needed space. Time.

Unfortunately, it didn't look as though Toby was going to give her either.

11

MADISON HADN'T SAID a word since they'd left his parents' house. She'd bid a polite farewell and thank you to his sister, sister-in-law and parents, and allowed him to lead her out to his car.

He wasn't sure what had changed. He couldn't tell if she was upset or angry. He was completely clueless to her mood and he wasn't planning on letting her keep him in the dark once they reached his house.

Of course, he hadn't asked her if she wanted to come back to his place; he was taking that choice out of her hands. If she wanted him to take her home after he got to the bottom of this strange shift in their relationship, he would. But he'd do everything he could to persuade her to stay first.

The second they pulled into his driveway, she spun towards him. "Why are we here? I want to go home."

"What's wrong?" Toby would prefer to start this conversation inside but it seemed Mad wasn't going to give him that option.

"Nothing. I told you I'm tired." She crossed her arms over her chest.

"I'm not taking you home until you talk to me." He turned off the car and removed the keys. "C'mon. I'll make us some coffee."

"I don't want coffee."

Angling his head away, he hid a smile. Her tone was sulky and for some reason he found it super cute. He figured Madison would not be impressed with his thoughts. "I want coffee."

He didn't really but it was an excuse to get her inside and at this point, short of picking her up and carrying her in like he had last night, he'd use anything at his disposal to get her into his house. Although, he wasn't ruling out a fireman hold just yet.

He'd climbed out and rounded the hood when her door flung open. "I don't drink coffee after three, it keeps me awake."

Toby smiled and held out his hand.

He didn't really care about her coffee preferences. The fact she was walking towards him and would soon follow him into the house was his only concern right now. When he got her inside, he'd find out what the problem was, fix it, then take her to bed.

He'd been waiting all day to peel her out of that sexy outfit she had on. It was some sort of all-in-one thing that he'd spent hours trying to work out how to remove. He wondered if there was a hidden zipper somewhere or if the bow at the back of her neck was the way to get it off.

However it came off, he wanted it on the floor of his bedroom at some point tonight. But first, he had a mood to figure out.

"If you don't want coffee, I can offer you wine."

"I don't drink."

He glanced over at Madison as they made their way up the path. "At all?"

"No." She shook her head. "I've never wanted to try it."

"You've never had *any*?" How was that possible?

She shrugged. "When all my peers were going to parties and getting drunk, I was too young, and by the time I was old enough I was busy studying."

She'd left something out of that explanation. He wasn't sure what but he knew that wasn't the whole story.

Toby knew she'd gone through school ahead of time, but it had never occurred to him that she wouldn't have experienced the same things he had in high school and university. Now that he put his mind to it, he could see the connection to her struggles to interact, to connect in certain situations.

While she was completely at home and in her element with the kids in her classes, she was stilted and abrupt or a silent bystander with adults. He'd seen it today. And now that she'd pointed him in the right direction, he completely understood why the change in mood this evening.

"Well, I think it's time you got an education in alcohol."

"Oh no. I don't think so." She tried to pull her hand from his. "I'm quite happy not drinking, thank you."

There was that prim-and-proper tone that revved his engine. Jesus, he was a sick fuck if her haughty manner got him off. If he were honest, he'd admit everything about her got him off.

Grinning at her, he unlocked the front door and ushered her inside. "Humor me. I want to see you try new things. You didn't have a problem with it last night." He winked and watched a gentle flush wash up her throat and into her cheeks.

"I...well...that's..." Madison sighed. "Fine. But only a taste."

"I'll accept that."

He threaded his fingers through hers and led her to the

kitchen. If he could convince her to try something new every day, he'd be a happy man. And he wasn't only talking about sexually. Although he would admit the idea of exploring new pleasures with her in bed was more than appealing, he also wanted to see her find pleasures outside the bedroom.

~

"THAT'S ENOUGH FOR YOU, LIGHTWEIGHT." Toby plucked the glass from her hand.

"Hey. I wasn't finished," Madison complained with a pout.

He chuckled. "You've had more than enough for a first attempt."

"But I really liked it." Was that her voice, all whiny and pleading? She sat up straight and her head went a little woozy. "Wow." Grabbing the edge of the couch, Madison tried to steady herself.

Smiling, Toby leaned over and whispered in her ear. "Feeling it now?"

She nodded. Big mistake. That dizzy sensation multiplied. "Oo…"

"Like I said. Lightweight."

"I barely had a glass."

"Actually, that's your second."

"Really?" Madison didn't remember finishing the first.

"Yep." He placed her glass on the side table next to his. "I think it's time for bed."

"Oh, of course. Right." She stood on unsteady legs. Was she drunk on less than two glasses of wine? "I'll call a cab…"

Toby laughed and scooped her into his arms, making her head spin for a whole different reason. "Not a chance. Bed. As in *my* bed, Ms. Tipsy-lightweight."

"Are you going to get me to try more new things?" she asked while snuggling her head into the side of Toby's neck. Heat rolled off him, making her want to get closer. "You're so warm and comfy."

"Jesus. I think you're a one-glass girl from now on." Toby entered his room and strode to the bed. Lowering her to the soft bedding, he hovered over her. "Can you get undressed yourself or do you need help?"

"Undress me." She went for sexy but when he smiled at her with humor, Madison figured she'd missed the mark. Sighing, she said, "I wish I was sexy."

Toby reared back. "What?"

She pouted. "I'm not sexy."

"Mad, you're one of the sexiest women I've ever known."

"No I'm not. You don't want to rip my clothes off all the time."

He made a sound that was a mix between a groan and laughter. "You have no idea."

"You *do* want to rip my clothes off?"

"Madison, I've spent the whole day with a semi."

"A semi what?"

The sound he made now was definitely a laugh. "Half a hard-on."

Half? "How do you have a half? Show me." She scrambled up and reached for his pants.

"Whoa. Wait."

"But I want to see. You're getting me to try new things, right? And I've never seen half a hard-on before. Actually, till last night, I'd never see a full one up close and personal."

"Fuck." he pushed her hands away and took a step back. "Let me do it, and we have to be quick."

"Why?"

"Because just the thought of you wanting to see my cock

gets me hard; actually showing it to you is guaranteed to have it standing at full-salute attention."

"Someone looking at you makes you aroused?"

He dropped his pants and Madison kept her eyes glued to his groin. She watched as the thick shaft that hung between his legs grew thicker and rose up until it almost brushed his stomach.

"Wow. You weren't wrong. That thing just stood right up." Reaching out, she caressed the steely length from base to tip.

"Mad," Toby growled, his hands fisting at his side.

"I want to suck it again."

"Fuck." He stepped back out of reach. "You're drunk."

She laughed. "I'm not that drunk." Tilting her head to the side, Madison considered his words. "Nope. Not drunk. A little mellow, definitely feeling less inhibited than normal, but not drunk."

"Christ, Mad, you're killing me."

"Why?"

"Because I'd love nothing more than to tumble you to the bed and let you suck me. To suck *you*. Lick you. Fuck you into next week."

She grinned. "That's what I want too."

"Not until you're sober." Toby crossed his arms over his wide chest and took another step away to punctuate his statement.

"Well, that's it. I'm never drinking again." Flopping back on the bed, she threw an arm over her eyes. "How long 'til I'm sober?"

"Morning."

Madison jack-knifed up. "What?"

"I'll fuck you in the morning and not before," he ground out.

She eyed him. A vein pulsed at the side of his forehead; a matching tic throbbed in his jaw. His eyes were black as night and his whole body was rigid, as though one touch and he'd snap.

One side of her mouth kicked up. It wouldn't take much to push him over the edge and get him to throw her down and fuck her.

She giggled. She'd never even thought of that word before Toby.

"What's funny?" he asked.

"I want you to *fuck* me." She laughed. "I can't believe I'm thinking that word, never mind saying it."

"Say it again and I'll give that suddenly dirty mouth something to shut it up."

"Promises, promises," she teased. Oh my god, where had that come from?

"Mad." The upward curl of his lips diminished Toby's warning tone.

"What word do you use to call my vagina?"

"What?" he gasped, his arms dropping to his sides.

"What—"

"I heard you. Why do you want to know?"

"Because I want to use it. I want to call that," she pointed at his erection, "a cock and this," she placed her hand over her crotch, "a..."

"Pussy. Cunt. Either works." He answered her but she could tell it was grudgingly.

"Okay." Madison reached up and undid the bow at the back of her neck. "I want you to put your cock in my cunt."

He pounced on her. She let out a scream before laughter bubbled in her chest, bursting from her throat.

Toby pinned her beneath him. "Are you going to put your cock in my cunt now?" she asked, batting her eyelashes.

"You've got a very bad girl hiding behind that prim-and-proper exterior."

"Do you like me bad?" Madison asked. She had to admit she kinda liked *being* bad. Especially with Toby. "Or do you like me good?"

"I like you any way I can get you."

"Well tonight I want to be bad." She stuck her tongue out and ran it along Toby's jaw, the friction from his stubble giving her a delicious shiver. "Be bad with me. Please?"

His eyes dilated. His nostrils flared. "How bad do you want to be, Mad?"

"As bad as you know how."

12

She wanted to be bad.

A glass and a half couldn't make her that drunk. He could start off slow, work up to the bad stuff, and by then she'd be sober and could easily say no, right?

He lowered his forehead to hers. "If I touch you and you don't like it, you have to tell me to stop."

"Okay."

"Did you like everything we did last night?"

"Yes." She nodded, her brow rubbing on his. "Absolutely."

"I need to know exactly what you've done before me." God, he didn't want to know about any other guys touching her but he needed that info if he was going to take her further than he already had.

"I had intercourse. Once."

"Once?" he choked out through his suddenly constricted throat.

"Four years ago."

Fuck. No wonder he'd hurt her when he'd rammed inside

that first time. He ground his teeth and asked the next question. "Did you come?"

"No."

"You'd never had an orgasm before last night?" Jesus Christ. He might not have been the one to tear through her hymen but he'd been the first in every other way. Pride swelled in his chest. After that initial fuck-up, he'd made sure it was good for her—and he'd make damn sure every time from now on was better.

"Not with a guy. I've given myself a few. They weren't anything like what you did though."

"You've masturbated?" Images rolled through his mind. Mad with her small fingers thrusting into her pussy, her thumb rubbing her clit. "I want to see you get yourself off."

He pushed up and climbed off the bed. Quickly, he got rid of the rest of his clothes then walked to the door and flicked on the overhead light.

"I want to be able to see your fingers clearly when you shove them up your cunt." He went with the more dirty term to see what reaction he got from Mad. When she shuddered and clamped her thighs together, he knew she liked it. "Strip."

"Now? You want me to masturbate *now*?" She sank her teeth into her bottom lip. "But I thought..."

Her eyes zeroed in on his hand working his cock as he walked back towards her. "I'm going to sit on the end of the bed, between your spread legs, and watch you come for me. Then I'm going to drag you to me and shove my cock in your soaking-wet cunt. You want me to do that, don't you, Mad?"

'Y-yes." The word hissed between her parted lips. Her eyelids lowered over her lust-filled eyes and her chest rose with each staggered breath.

"Then strip. Fuck yourself with your fingers for me."

In a blur of motion, Madison shimmied out of her clothes

and sent them flying. In seconds she was naked, legs spread wide, hand buried in her slick folds in front of him.

"Fuck that's hot." He moved to the end of the bed and kneeled between her feet. He didn't dare get any closer. Not if he wanted her to get off before he jumped her. "Let me hear you too, baby. I want all those sexy sounds you make when you come."

He watched and listened. Stroked his cock and prayed for strength. It didn't take her long to reach the point of orgasm. Toby couldn't remember seeing anything as hot as Mad thrusting her fingers in and out of her pussy. She manipulated her clit on every third or fourth plunge and he quickly worked out she was trying to prolong her release, pushing herself higher and higher but not over.

She might not have experienced pleasure with a man but she certainly knew how to find it on her own.

"That's it. Take more." Toby squeezed his cock as a shudder went through him. If she didn't go off soon he'd be blowing all over the bed. "Deeper. Harder."

"Toby." Madison gasped. Trembled. Bucked. "Oh god. I'm…"

"Yes. Yes." He rose up, moved closer and, as she flew over the ledge, he pulled her hand away and shoved himself inside her spasming pussy. "Yes!"

She wrapped her legs around his waist, her heels digging into his spine, and surged up to meet him as he pounded into her. He wouldn't last long and had no hope of getting her to go with him but he'd be sure to make it up to her later.

Wet heat coated him from root to tip. Slick walls sucked at him as she continued to contract with her waning release.

Muscles strained. Sweat popped out of every pore. And still he pounded into her. Clenching his jaw he used every ounce of strength to hold off the orgasm boiling in his balls. He slid his hands under her back, curled his hands around her shoulders and held her in place while he drove his hips forward. Harder. Faster.

Ramming every single inch of his cock in and out of Mad's tight pussy became his only focus. His gut tightened a split-second before his balls contracted and he went off like a rocket. Jet after jet of come exploded from his cock as he kept up the hard driving pace of impaling her.

"Toby!"

He barely registered Mad's cry, too consumed by the punishing grip of her wet cunt as she came again.

MADISON STRUGGLED to draw in air. Toby's weight crushed her as his spent body collapsed on top of her. With a grunt, he pushed off, flipping them over and reversing their positions. Once again he showed superior strength by keeping their bodies joined throughout the maneuver.

For long moments the only sound was their harsh breaths. Last night they'd done some amazing things and she had some spectacular orgasms, but tonight... Her whole body tingled and little ripples of pleasure continued to roll out from her pussy.

God. She couldn't believe she'd been brave enough to use those words. And when Toby used them...she trembled with a strong aftershock. She'd climaxed twice and still felt on edge. Being this aroused, for this long, was an eye-opening experience.

"Jesus. You're insatiable," Toby murmured into her hair.

"It's your fault." Finally drawing in a deep breath, she tilted her head back and gazed at him. "Never like this until you."

He grinned. One that said he was more than pleased with that piece of information.

She smiled and wiggled her hips.

Toby's mouth thinned, and his gaze turned from happy to worried.

Her insides clenched. "What?"

"Are you on the pill?"

"Why—?" *Oh god.* "N-no."

He closed his eyes. "Shit. I'm sorry."

They hadn't used protection. She could feel how wet she was. Way wetter than she could ever get on her own. *Think. Think.* Where was she in her cycle?

"Fuck." Gripping her hips, Toby lifted her off his cock and, wrapping his arms around her, turned them on their sides. "It never entered my mind. I've *never* done that before. I'm clean. You've got not worries there."

"It's okay." She'd always been regular and she was sure she was due next week. In two days, in fact. "Obviously I'm clean and I know nothing is one hundred percent certain but I'm out of the danger zone. I'll know Monday."

His gaze searched hers.

Cupping his face, Madison brushed her thumb over his bottom lip. "If we have sex again, we'll be more careful."

"If? There's no if. I plan to be inside you as often as you'll let me. You wanted to be bad, remember."

She smiled. "Yeah."

"So you should go on the pill. Just to be sure. I'll still use condoms but it's best to have double protection. In case."

Wow. Okay. Asking her to go on oral contraception was a long-term-relationship thing. "What are you saying?"

"This isn't a one-time thing."

"Well, no. We've had sex more than once already."

"Don't get cute, Mad, you know what I mean."

"No, actually, I don't. This is one of those new experiences you're helping me try. You're going to have to spell it out for me. I might be intelligent but this type of thing is not within my educational scope."

"Okay. Shooting straight."

"That would be good. No chance of misunderstandings then."

"We're together. A couple. Exclusive. You don't date anyone else. I don't date anyone else."

"What about work? It will get awkward if anyone finds out. We have to keep it quiet. No one needs to know what we do outside of school hours." The thought of any of their colleagues, or worse, the students, finding out sent a cold shiver down her spine. Madison was certain there was some type of no-fraternization clause in her contract. She couldn't remember the exact words though. As soon as she got home she'd check.

Toby frowned. "I don't want to hide like we're some sort of dirty secret."

"Not a dirty one, just...I'm new at Huntington. I don't want to lose my job—"

"What the fuck? Why would us dating get you fired?"

She shrugged. "I don't know that it would but I don't want to start any kind of gossip or innuendo, especially among the students. There are enough rumors running through the halls without adding myself to them. Plus I need to check my contract. I remember something in there about no-fraternizing."

He was quiet for a moment, causing her heart to beat double-time. "Fine. We keep it on the down-low at work."

Planting a quick kiss on his lips, she pulled back and smiled. "Thank you. I'll make an appointment with my doctor on Monday."

The smile Toby gave her curled her toes and made her lower belly flutter. "Okay, bad girl, let's take a shower."

Like he had many times over the last two days, he scooped

her up in his arms and carried her to the bathroom. "You know carting me around all the time is going to do your back in."

Toby laughed. A deep guttural sound that shook his body and rumbled through the air. "You're lighter than a tackle bag and I cart those around every day, so I'm more than conditioned to indulge in this pleasurable activity."

"You like carrying me?"

"Love it." He planted a smacking kiss on her mouth. "Now. Time to get bad in the shower."

Madison smiled. "What do you have in mind?"

"You're going to put your hands on the wall, spread your legs and tilt that gorgeous ass up so I can play."

A shudder racked her. "Play?"

"We're going to get *real* dirty, bad girl, are you up for that?"

"I..."

"Remember, anything you don't like or that hurts, you say stop, I stop."

"Okay."

"Right." He lowered her feet to the floor. "Turn around and palm the wall."

Quivering all over, Madison turned and placed her hands on the wall. "Is this okay?"

"Wider." Toby nudged her feet farther apart then put his hands on her hips and guided her movements. "Angle your pelvis and arch your back...yeah, that's it."

His hand swept down her spine, making her shiver.

She glanced over her shoulder to see Toby drop to his knees behind her and get a close-up look at her exposed flesh. Shuddering, she closed her eyes and moaned.

"Hold that wall, Mad. I'm going to make you come hard."

Then he put his mouth on her. Put his fingers in her. He stroked and licked. Nipped and sucked. She whimpered and moaned. Sobbed and cried out. But he didn't let her go over.

With ruthless determination, Toby kept her riding the edge of release for long, torturous minutes.

Breath sobbing from her lungs, body straining in desperation, Madison begged for more. And when he took his mouth away and rose to his feet behind her, she screamed in release as he drove his cock into her eager pussy.

13

TOBY SHUDDERED. He'd barely gotten the condom on before he drove himself inside Mad's clenching pussy. God, she did his head in. Totally stripped him of control. He had no willpower when it came to her.

Buried deep, he held still and waited for her orgasm to ease. The tight clamp of her pussy wouldn't let him build up a steady rhythm until the sharp edge smoothed out and her muscles went lax.

He wrapped an arm around her waist and held her against him. They were both slick with sweat and breathing hard. The echo of her scream still rang in his ears and he wanted to hear her go off like that again. Wanted to take her up hard and fast, but this time he wanted to hear her scream his name.

Scooting his hand down between her legs, Toby ran his fingers through her wetness, making sure he got his skin good and covered. Straightening, he gripped her hip in one hand and slid his wet fingers into the crease of her ass.

With gentle rocks of his hips, he dragged his cock through the swollen folds of her pussy and pressed his slick fingers against the puckered opening of her ass. She mewled, thrusting backwards, eager for the tantalizing pleasure he offered.

She'd enjoyed the anal play they'd indulged in last night but he'd only got to the first knuckle with two fingers then. Tonight he was going in with three and sinking them as deep as he could.

He'd fuck her slowly, with his cock and his fingers, filling her up, and taking her over the next peak at the same time as he dove off it.

She pushed back harder as he pressed in. "You okay?" he asked, needing to know she was good with what he was doing.

"Mmm…" Her ass tilted higher, her body softening around his fingers.

Fuck.

She was his wet dream come to life. Sweet, innocent, prim-and-proper Madison Keibler liked it in the ass. Toby vibrated in anticipation. She'd taken to this dark pleasure like a duck to water and if she kept going, he'd be able to sink his cock into her tighter-than-tight rear sooner rather than later.

"More." She rocked into him.

Increasing the pressure, he watched two fingers slide through the tight ring of muscle until they disappeared completely inside her. He groaned. Rolled his hips and fucked her pussy with a couple of short thrusts.

Arching towards him, she hissed, "Yes…"

She gripped him, ass and pussy, and Toby prayed he had the strength to hold off his building release. Withdrawing his fingers, he added a third and pushed back in. It was more constricted but she took him all the way in with one excruciating, ball-twisting stroke.

Keeping a grip on his control was proving impossible. He didn't need to move, Mad did that herself. Back and forth, she propelled her hips and slowly fucked him. Toby was under no illusions about who was in charge here. She had complete and utter control.

"Toby." His name slipped from her lips on a moan.

"Right here, Mad. Take what you need, baby."

"More." Her body quivered around him. "I need...more."

"How much more?" Did she want...? His balls ached, his cock throbbed as she worked it in and out of her pussy.

"Harder."

Fuck. This woman was going to kill him. "Are you sure?"

She showed him how sure she was by driving her hips against him hard and fast. A cry of pleasure tore from her throat and she retreated, only to slam back again.

Toby attempted to call her name but the ecstasy ripping through him as she impaled herself on his cock and fingers again and again squeezed his vocal cords, turning any noises he tried to make into garbled groans.

With each plunge of her body over his, they climbed. The jagged edge of his orgasm sliced into him and there was no way he could remain passive in their lovemaking any longer.

He started slow, rocking into her rhythm, until he overtook her and kicked the pace up another gear. She followed. Eagerly kept up and urged him on. They came together hard. They came together fast. And with each advance and retreat, wicked lust speared him.

Savage arousal like he'd never known whipped through him.

The sounds of their bodies slamming together, the grunts and moans and groans, combined with the driving beat and delivered a soundtrack of passion and pleasure that only increased his need.

"Touch your clit," he growled. There was no way he could do it without losing their rhythm and he needed her to come.

Needed to feel her squeeze him to the point of pain before he took the plunge and blew his load.

As soon as Mad put her hand between her legs, her fingertips brushing his shaft with every stroke, she clenched down on him. For one breath-stopping moment, Toby felt held in suspended animation—then she broke.

Her orgasm gripped her whole body in bone-shaking convulsions that sucked him in and threw him over the edge. Gasping, punching, roaring, Toby followed her into the madness.

MADISON WOKE to aching muscles and a dry throat. Opening her eyes, she stared at the unfamiliar wall. A soft snore wheezed behind her and it all came flooding back. Everything.

Every single second of last night and what she'd allowed Toby to do.

What she'd all but begged him to do.

No. She *had* begged. Over and over and over again.

Heat engulfed her. She couldn't decide if it was embarrassment or remembered pleasure. Emotions overwhelmed her. Happiness, satisfaction, passion, delight, anguish, pride, want, need, unease, dread, fear, shame—panic. The sentiments tumbled and collided and tangled and confused.

Her stomach rolled, nausea swamped, cramped her.

She needed to think. Couldn't do that here, in Toby's bed. Spotting his shirt on the floor, Madison slid out of bed without disturbing him and, grabbing the top, she made her way out of his room.

A shower would be great right now. Hard to collect her

thoughts and decide what to do when she smelled like Toby—like sex. Dirty, dirty, hot sex.

Trembling, she placed a hand on her lower stomach and pressed. But the action didn't stop the ripples of pleasure working their way through her.

He'd given her more than she'd asked for. He'd offered and she took. And she gave. There was nothing she wouldn't have done for him during their night of passion. Madison had the strong suspicion Toby could make her do anything with just a look, a smile.

Having no parameters for this...*whatever* it was, she couldn't determine if her behavior—her emotions—were normal.

For the second time in two days, Madison found herself wishing for a friend to confide in. Slipping Toby's shirt over her head, she wound her way through his house until she came to the living room. The view here was a little different from that in the bathroom but no less spectacular. A huge deck with a group of comfortable-looking lounges and chairs drew her.

She opened the sliding glass door and stepped out into the crisp morning air. Too early for much activity, there were only a few sailboats bobbing their way across the water. Choosing the lounger with the most sweeping view, Madison curled up on the soft cushions.

How had she found herself here?

The man inside had stormed her defenses and made himself at home and it scared the life out of her. Madison was under no illusions that Toby returned her depth of emotion. She was also well aware that what she was feeling could possibly be a byproduct of the uninhibited passion she experienced with him.

He was vibrancy, life, all about a good time.

She was staid, serious, on the fringes of a world she often didn't understand.

How could they have more than sex?

They couldn't. No matter how much—how deep—she thought her feelings for Toby went, they couldn't, wouldn't, last. Opposites might attract but the things that attracted more often than not repelled in the end.

And that heart she'd claimed never to have had broken... Madison trembled with the knowledge that Toby would be the one to shatter it into a million pieces when they were done.

She couldn't trust the feelings of affection currently zipping through her. The only thing real between them was the passion, the pleasure—everything else was a consequence of their unbridled desire.

It was chemical.

Pheromones and endorphins.

A biological cocktail guaranteed to deliver rapture and encourage them to come together again and again. The way the human race had done from the beginning of time. Procreate or perish.

Madison wasn't sure how long she'd lain there deep in thought when Toby crouched beside her.

"Hey." He offered a smile. Not his usual all-is-great one. This one held a tinge of concern that her stupid heart wanted to latch on to.

"Hi."

He brushed a lock of hair off her shoulder. "Couldn't sleep?"

"Not once I'm awake."

"You could have woken me."

She didn't bother to tell him she hadn't wanted to. He knew.

"You're thinking too hard again."

"I can't help it. There's a lot to sort out."

"Didn't we do that last night?" Was that a flicker of fear in his eyes?

"I..." What? What did she want or need to go through?

"Mad." He brushed his lips across her temple. "Come inside. I'll make us some breakfast."

Standing, he offered his hand. Everything inside her wanted to take that hand and hold on. Could she do that and survive when he walked away? Would she regret not spending whatever time they had together if she ended it now?

She'd agreed to go on the pill. That was a long-term commitment, but was that really what he wanted from her or was it just the sex? Too many questions and no answers readily available. She couldn't go to the library and look them up either. Her go-to method of working through a problem was no longer an option.

"One moment at a time, Mad, one *day* at a time. Right now it's breakfast. Toast, eggs, coffee."

"And after?"

"Well..." He glanced up at the clear blue sky. "It's a nice day. We could put the top down and take a drive along the coast. Stop somewhere for lunch."

Swallowing, she placed her hand in his. For all her fear and apprehension, she couldn't deny herself more time with him. And in spite of the spectacular sex, it wasn't only the physical way he made her feel that drew her. He enticed her away from the fringes and pulled her into the middle of living.

She couldn't walk away from that—or him—yet.

"You're going to cook me breakfast?" she asked as he led her inside.

"You doubt my culinary expertise?"

"Um..."

He directed her to take a seat at the counter dividing the kitchen from the living room. "Prepare to eat those doubts."

Toby had proven his athleticism transferred to the bedroom and now he showed her he was as agile, just as efficient, in the kitchen. He chopped, scrambled, and spread with steady hands and sure motions. His movements were purely masculine and yet he performed a job that traditionally fell to the female gender.

Even the pink apron he wore over his boxer briefs didn't detract from his maleness. When he'd first tied that on, she'd had to choke back a laugh. Now she was intrigued as to why he had the completely feminine apparel.

"Where did you get the apron?"

He glanced over with a grin. "Cassie."

"Ah."

"Yeah. Nothing like a little sister to punch holes in your ego."

"Why wear it?"

Putting a plate of yummy-smelling food in front of her, he said, "I don't own any others, and there's no point buying one when I've got a perfectly functional one."

Madison realized the color wasn't even a consideration for him. He was so comfortable in his own skin, in his masculinity, wearing a pink apron didn't even make him blink.

In that moment, she envied him his confidence. The only place she'd ever been that sure of herself was in the classroom, and life was so much more than that. Toby was right. She needed to try new things. Push her boundaries, overcome her discomfort and live.

And right now, the place she felt most alive was with him.

14

TOBY LEANED against the wall and watched Madison paw her way through the on-sale knick-knacks. He'd driven south and they'd ended up in a little coastal town with lots of tourist-type shops and eateries. They'd devoured a fresh seafood lunch and were now 'walking off' the calories.

It had been a great day so far. The weather was perfect, not too hot even when the sun beat down on their heads. A beautiful autumn day enjoyed with a beautiful woman.

"Oh, Toby, look." Mad turned towards him holding up a little figurine he couldn't see from his position. "You should get this for your sister."

Pushing off the wall, he walked over and cupped her outstretched hand in both of his. Even the innocent touch got his blood humming.

She held a gorgeous porcelain figurine. A mother knelt on the floor, a small child in front of her, and they were finger painting. The woman even looked like his sister, with her sweeping brown hair and mischievous grin.

Mad was right. It fit Cassie to a T.

"You need something different for Shaye." She put the figurine in his hands and went back to searching the shelves. "Here. What about this?"

This time she held out a couple. The man held the woman in his arms, his hands splayed over her swollen belly. Problem was, the woman had blonde curls cascading over her shoulders and made him think of Madison, not his pregnant sister-in-law. Clearing his constricting throat, he asked, "What else is there?"

She frowned. "You're right. This isn't Shaye at all."

As she moved on, he picked up the rejected man-and-woman figurine. "I'll just get them to wrap the one for Cassie while you keep looking."

"Okay."

Too busy to look his way, Mad didn't see him take both figurines to the sales counter.

He got the girl behind the counter to wrap the man and woman first then the mother and child. Spotting a beautiful blown-glass bowl he thought his mother would love, he asked the sales clerk to wrap that too before making his way back to Mad.

She'd moved over to the far shelves. For a moment he just observed her while she studied the items in front of her. Even deep in thought, she was beautiful. The sight of her thrummed through him and kicked up his heart rate, tightening his groin.

Would that soul-deep tug ever go away or would she always inspire this dark need inside him?

"I've found a couple of things that might work..."

Toby smiled. She was so serious about her search. He was sure she was enjoying herself but there was that thread of earnest concentration, as though the weight of the world rested on the outcome.

"Show me."

The first ornament she handed him was a couple lying on a picnic blanket, a baby sleeping between them. Instantly he thought of Coop and Shaye. "This one."

She grinned at him. "Yeah, that's my pick too."

"What else you got?"

"Oh, this baby in a crib." She held it up, tipped her head to the side and considered it thoughtfully. "Mom and dad aren't quite right."

He studied the figurine. "Hmm... You're right. Not Coop and Shaye." Putting that one back on the shelf, he said, "I found a glass bowl for my mom, help me find something for Granny."

"Oh. I know the perfect thing!" Mad darted around the end of the shelves into the next isle and Toby's face broke out in a huge smile. She was having fun—almost childlike in her delight. Then again, from what he knew about her life, fun appeared to be a foreign concept.

He planned to make sure she enjoyed herself more often in the future. Following after her, they bumped into each other as she came rushing back his way.

"This." She held up a figurine similar to the ones they'd picked for his sisters; they were probably by the same artist. This one had an old woman, knitting cradled in her lap, while she sat in a wooden rocking chair. "Perfect, right?" Mad asked.

While the others were all porcelain, this one was a combination of wood, porcelain and fabric. The blanket the woman knitted was soft against his fingertips and the spindles of the chair back were smooth, exactly like the ones his Gramps made.

It amazed him how much Mad 'got' his family after meeting them only once. Did she see him as clearly? Did he want her to?

"Is that it? Do you need to get anything else?"

"Nope. That'll do for now. Do you want to keep looking around while I pay for everything?"

"I might slip next door and grab a drink. Do you want something?"

"Sure. A bottle of water would be good."

"Okay. Meet you out front."

Again Toby found himself standing still and watching her. Before, he'd been intrigued. He'd been attracted. Now he was in serious like. Each new facet of Madison he uncovered was more appealing than the last. He wanted to discover all the sides to her. Wanted to be with her when she experienced something new, found joy in the world around her.

It was like watching a flower bloom, and the more she opened, the more beautiful she became.

Toby slowly pulled in a breath. He was in deep. Far deeper than he thought possible, and he didn't know what to do about it. Where did they go from here?

This morning he'd told her one moment at a time—one day at a time. He should take his own advice and appreciate the moments and stop worrying about the future.

TOBY'S PHONE rang through the car speakers, breaking the comfortable silence they'd fallen into as they drove down the highway. The top was up because when they'd left the sleepy town they'd had lunch in, clouds had been rolling in from the south and he didn't want to risk getting rained on or having to pull over. They'd made good time, and were only a few minutes for the turnoff.

Hitting a button on the steering wheel, he answered the call. "Hey, Dad."

"Your sister's in the hospital. According to your mother, things are moving fast. Get here as soon as you can."

The line went dead. Toby chuckled. "Right. Well. Things are a little tense, I think."

"It's the first grandchild, right?"

"Yep."

"I expect everyone's a little nervous then." Envy stabbed her. He had such a large, close family. "Are you?"

"What's there to be nervous about? I get to be the favorite uncle. The one who sneaks the kid chocolate and teaches him to swear."

She gasped. "You can't do that!"

Toby laughed. "I'm joking."

"Oh."

He reached over and grabbed her hand. "Looks like today's the day. Good thing we picked up a present."

"Yes." Glancing out the side window, Madison thought about all the things she'd never had that he took for granted. His brothers and his sister. His parents and grandparents. The large extended family she'd met only yesterday. People who loved him, who wanted to spend time with him, surrounded Toby. Cassie's baby would have that too.

"Hey." He squeezed her hand. "You okay?"

"I'm fine. Just thinking. If it's out of the way to drop me home first, I'll get a cab from the hospital so you can be with your family quicker."

"Oh no, you're not going home and leaving me to pace the halls on my own."

"You won't be alone. You'll have your whole family around you."

Toby pulled her hand to his mouth and pressed his lips to her knuckles. "But I want *you* there with me."

"But I'm not family, and I'm sure Cassie would prefer not

to have strangers hanging around." She didn't want a repeat of yesterday's disconnected feeling.

"Pretty sure Cassie wouldn't care if the Queen was waiting for her to give birth. At this point, it's probably Luc she doesn't want to lay eyes on."

Madison smiled. "Poor Luc. I've read that a woman in labor can be especially nasty to their baby's father."

Toby chuckled. "Somehow I think Luc can handle anything Cassie dishes out. Lord knows she hasn't managed to scare him off yet. And she's tried."

A part of her wanted to be there with his family, waiting for the birth of their newest member. But she couldn't shake the feeling that she didn't belong, shouldn't be intruding on what ought to be a private moment for the Morelands.

Before she could decide either way, Toby turned into the parking station of one of Sydney's largest hospitals. "That call came in at the right moment. Another five minutes and we'd have had to double back. With any luck, we'll be one of the first ones here."

Resigned to going in with him, Madison decided she'd give it ten minutes and if she felt like an intruder, she'd slip away and grab a taxi to take her home.

He found a parking space quickly and in minutes they were walking through the front doors of the hospital and looking for the information board. Toby held her hand and tugged her over to an elderly woman wearing what looked like a uniform. Her nametag informed them she was Renata, a patient get-well ambassador.

Madison wasn't sure what a patient get-well ambassador was, or whether she'd be any help, but as there didn't appear to be any place to ask questions or a display with the information they needed, they couldn't be in worse shape after seeking her out.

"Hi. Can you point us in the direction of the labor department, please?" Toby asked.

"Last bank of lifts. Sixth floor." Renata shuffled away before they could question her further.

"Well. I guess we're on our own." Toby smiled and squeezed her hand. "I'm going to hazard a guess that she means the elevators at the end of this hallway. C'mon. It can't be too hard to find the right way."

After two wrong turns and a dead end, they finally found not only the elevators, but an information board that told them to take the lift to the sixth floor.

"See. Not so hard." He grinned as he pressed the up button.

The doors opened immediately and Toby ushered her in with a hand to her back. Madison leaned into the touch. In the past, she would have jumped away from such physical contact. After spending days with him caressing her in more intimate ways, she was unable to deny the yearning that grabbed her whenever he brushed against her, never mind when he laid a hand on her completely.

Hitting the number six button, Toby turned to face her. "Okay, what's your bet? Boy or girl?"

"You don't know? I thought you said 'him' in the car."

"Oh, I did. I'm hoping for a boy just so we can continue to outnumber Cassie, but I'd also like to see Luc cope with a precious princess. I've heard stories about the time Cassie made him help her run a little girl's birthday party, and legend says he looks good in a crown."

"Ah..." Madison wasn't sure what to make of Toby's comments. Was he joking around? The smile on his lips said he was, but she wasn't used to banter of this kind. It was one of the reasons she'd struggled at his family's barbeque yesterday. She just didn't know how to respond to this type of conversation.

"I suppose the important thing is that mom and bub are healthy," he added as the lift rose.

"I would think that would be the best outcome."

He glanced at her quizzically. "Hmm..."

A bell dinged, the car came to a stop and the doors swished open. Stepping out, Madison was immediately confronted with a corridor overflowing with people. "Oh my."

Toby laughed. "And the Morelands have arrived."

They'd arrived all right. It was standing-room only, and no way was anyone moving from where they stood. "Do you think they'll throw everyone out? Surely you aren't allowed to have this many visitors."

He slung his arm around her shoulders and pulled her snug against him. "I'm sure Granny will put some order into this mess in a few minutes. She's been marshaling the family since before I was born."

"All these people aren't blood related, are they?"

Toby stretched to his toes and peered over the crowd. "Yep. Looks like they are."

"How many of you are there?" This was so different from her little family of three.

"Let's see..." He took a moment to think. "With all the Moreland cousins, twenty-three, last time we counted."

"Soon to be twenty-four."

"Twenty-five, if we count Shaye and Coop's coming bundle of joy, and really, we have to." He smiled at her. "And that includes Zac's fiancé too. Freddie's not officially a Moreland yet but it's a done deal."

"Wow." Twenty-five immediate family members? "That's a lot of presents to buy at Christmas." Madison couldn't even fathom having to buy that many gifts.

The thought was thrilling and intimidating in equal

measure. What must it be like to have that many relatives? That many people to love and be loved by? She hoped Toby never took that for granted.

Madison knew she wouldn't, if she were lucky enough to have a big loving family like the Morelands.

15

TOBY STARED down at the sleeping bundle in his arms. Bennett Lucas Wilhelm was a strapping nine pound, eight ounces and twenty-five inches long. He was a monster. And while Cassie wasn't small, Toby had no idea where she'd hidden this guy or how she'd managed to give birth to him.

"God, Cassie," he whispered in awe. "You're amazing."

His sister laughed tiredly. "I'm pretty amazed myself. He's perfect, isn't he?"

"You have to ask?" Toby glanced up. "He looks like a mini Luc."

"Yeah, well, there's the downside right there," mumbled the proud dad.

Toby smiled at them both. "You guys really did good." He looked back at his nephew. "Hard to believe this is what we've all been waiting months for."

"Is that a tear in your eye, big brother?" Cassie asked.

"Maybe one," he conceded. "But only one." Turning to Mad standing quietly at his side, he moved closer. "Here. Have a hold."

"Oh no. I couldn't." She backed away a step.

"Of course you can." He followed her.

"But—"

Toby placed Bennett against her chest, giving her no choice but to take him in her arms.

"Oh!" As he lowered his nephew's weight into Mad's arms, her face soften, her eyes took on a dreamy cast and her mouth tipped up in a beautiful smile as she gazed at the miracle in her arms. "He's heavier than I thought he'd be."

"He is on the large end of the scales," Cassie explained. "Weight, length, head circumference. All above average."

"Well, you chose to breed with a monster," Toby said over his shoulder, his gaze on Luc, who at six feet five was not a small man. His brother-in-law grinned.

"I've never held a baby before."

Mad's whispered words had Toby swinging his gaze back to her. "Never?"

"No." She shook her head. "I've never known anyone who had one."

How could she have gone her entire life without knowing anyone with a baby? "That seems completely strange to me. I know you have no siblings but surely a cousin, friend, neighbor, someone you've worked with..."

"No. This is the first baby I've been this close to."

"What?" How could she have lived such a sheltered life? "We should go down to the nursery to have a look at more."

"Why?"

"New experiences, remember?" There were so many other amazing things he wanted to show her. But right now he was going to stand here and enjoy the wonder on her face as she held his nephew.

She met his gaze, hers swimming with so many emotions he couldn't decipher them. "W-we should go. Let them rest."

"Okay." He took Bennett and walked him over to the new mom and dad. "We're going to go and let everyone else come in for a peek."

"Thanks for coming, Toby." Luc held out his hand.

Toby shook with his brother-in-law. "No. Thank *you* for wrangling this one." He tilted his chin towards Cassie.

"Ha ha."

"Call if you need anything." He placed a kiss on his sister's forehead. "I love you."

"Love you too." Cassie pushed him away. "Now get out of here. Bennett has the rest of his loyal subjects to greet yet."

Toby grinned. "You know Mom and Granny have everyone lined up in order of appearance, right?"

Cassie's mouth dropped open. "They do not?"

"Oh, yes they do. Coop and Shaye are next in line."

Luc chuckled. "In more ways than one."

"I still can't believe out of all of you, Cooper was the one to get a girl knocked up. I swear, we always thought it would be you."

"Me?" *What the fuck?*

"Yeah, well, in your playing days, there was always a bevy of women hanging around. We were sure either you'd fuck up or one would trap you."

His sister's comment immediately brought to mind last night and the one time in his life he'd forgotten to use protection. He'd never lost control that completely before.

And while Mad assured him they were probably safe, after holding his nephew...Toby wasn't so sure he wanted to be.

"EVER WALKED on the beach at sunset?"

Madison turned to look at Toby. "No."

"Okay. New experience coming up." He changed lanes then moved into the right-hand turn lane at the next set of lights.

They'd been quiet since leaving the hospital. Both of them lost in their own thoughts after being witness to the miracle of life. Madison couldn't get over the way she'd felt while holding little Bennett. She'd never thought about babies—in terms of her own or anyone else's. But holding that little man in her arms had triggered something.

She'd felt a yearning to hold him forever, and when Toby had taken him back, her arms felt empty and sadness over his loss filled her. She finally understood the concept of a woman's biological clock.

"You okay over there?"

"Just thinking about Bennett." It wasn't a complete lie.

"He's a cutie, that's for sure. And I can tell he's going to be trouble already."

"How?"

"Well, he's got the Moreland brothers for uncles, which on its own is trouble, but add in Cassie and oh boy, that little guy is going to be into everything and spoiled rotten."

Madison smiled. "I'm sure your parents and grandparents will have a lot to do with the spoiling. How long before Shaye's baby is born?"

"Um... August, I think. Bennett gets to have center stage all to himself for a few months yet."

The Moreland family was expanding rapidly.

Would her and Toby be adding to it?

She couldn't believe how blasé she'd been with regard to them forgetting protection. Now, after seeing firsthand what the result could be, she couldn't stop thinking about it.

"Here we are. Looks like we've got the place pretty much to

ourselves." Toby parked his car and switched it off. "Leave your shoes."

She'd worn flip-flops so it wasn't any trouble to slip them off and leave them behind.

"C'mon." Toby opened his door and climbed out.

Doing the same, Madison joined him on the path that led to the beach and slid her hand in his. "It's a beautiful night," she murmured.

"Yeah, there's a storm coming though." He pointed to the right. "Probably another couple of hours away but it'll definitely hit tonight."

They walked in silence for several minutes, the quiet and Toby's hand wrapped around hers comforting. The cool sand shifted beneath her feet, wiggled between her toes, and she glanced back a couple of times to see the tracks they left behind.

"Ever thought about having kids before?"

Madison's hand jerked in Toby's, her gaze swinging to his face. He remained facing forward but his fingers tightened around hers in a gentle squeeze. "No."

"But you're thinking about it now." He gave her another reassuring squeeze. "Me too."

"Do you want kids?" She asked one of the questions weighing on her mind since leaving his sister.

"Definitely. And I want them to have what I had growing up."

"A big family." She understood why. Knew if she'd been able to choose, she would have chosen a family like Toby's. "What you had, still have, is such an alien concept to what I know."

"You didn't grow up with friends from large families?"

"I didn't grow up with friends. Unless you count librarians and library staff or my parents' peers."

"And that's a completely alien concept to *me*. I can't even begin to imagine what your life was like. It sounds lonely."

"I guess it was in a way." She shrugged. "But it was all I knew for years I didn't really notice the loneliness so much as the differences between myself and others I'd come in contact with."

"I don't mean to sound rude or mean but your parents sound very cold."

"They are, and you're not. Being rude." She took a deep breath. Let it out through her mouth slowly. "I wasn't planned, and I'm pretty sure they never wanted a child. They certainly didn't know what to do with one. To them, I was just another student, one they had to teach twenty-four-seven."

"There's more to life than textbook learning." Toby stopped walking and spun her into his arms. "I want to teach you all the things you missed out on. I want to show you everything you've missed."

"Why?" Did he feel sorry for her? He shouldn't. While she'd missed a lot, she hadn't gone without, and, even if she sometimes felt like she was on the outside of life looking in, she was content. Most of the time.

"Because watching your face light up with pleasure, watching the wonder in your eyes when something feels good or makes you happy, is the greatest thing I've ever witnessed, and I want to see it every day."

"Oh."

"So here's the plan. Every day, I'll have a new experience for you. It could be an activity or a food or a drink or...I don't know. Whatever I can come up with."

"Something new every day?" He wanted to give her what she tried to give her students, except on a grander scale.

"Yep. And if I can fit in more than one each day, I will."

Madison smiled. "I'd like that."

"Good. Ready for your next new experience?"

"Sure."

"Considering you've never walked along the beach at sunset, I'm going to assume you haven't been kissed senseless on the beach at sunset either." He grinned as he lowered his head to hers.

The kiss started off sweet. Light brushes of his lips on hers. Then he pressed a little harder, swept his tongue along her bottom lip before urging her to open by probing at the seam between. As he took them deeper, he held her close, his arms a warm band around her waist.

Just as Madison's need for more edged towards urgency, Toby took them deeper still. One hand moved to her hip, the other slid up her back to tangle in her hair at the back of her neck. With a sharp tug on her hair, he tilted her head the way he wanted and drove his tongue hard and faster into her mouth. Their tongues stroked in a wet slide of heat and she dug her fingers into his shoulders as desire rushed to her sex.

Gasping for breath, he pulled back, separated their mouths and placed his brow on hers. "Jesus. You drive me mad."

"That's a two-way street."

"The plan was to walk on the beach, kiss for a bit before getting some dinner and then taking you home, with a kiss goodnight on your doorstep. That *was* the plan."

"And that's changed?"

"I can't touch you without wanting to get inside you."

"I don't see the problem." And she didn't. After that kiss, he could strip her naked now and take her on the beach for anyone to see and she wouldn't care. Okay, she'd care, but not until they were both lying in a sweaty heap of satisfied flesh. But if they couldn't do that here... "Take me home now."

His eyes searched hers.

"Toby, take me home and touch me."

He made a strangled sound in the back of his throat, and in a move too quick to see, he let her go and dropped his shoulder to her middle, lifting her into the air.

"Next new experience. Being carried in a classic fireman's hold by your boyfriend."

Boyfriend? Madison laughed. "I don't have a boyfriend."

Toby slapped her ass.

"Hey!"

"Lies." He rubbed his hand over the stinging area of her backside. "You most definitely *do* have a boyfriend."

I have a boyfriend. Laughter bubbled up her throat as she sung those four words over and over in head. *I have a boyfriend.*

Tobias Moreland was her boyfriend.

16

TOBY SMILED as he spotted Mad walking towards him. "Hey."

She startled, her stride jerking abruptly, before she moved past him with a frosty, "Mr. Moreland."

What the fuck? He glanced over his shoulder at her. That was the fifth time this week she'd given him the freeze-you-to-the-floor brushoff. Turning back to Jim Landry, Toby said, "At training this afternoon, let me know if you need extra work."

"Okay. Thanks, Sir."

Spinning around, Toby headed along the hall after Mad, accelerating his pace to catch up with her before she disappeared on him. They were going to have a little chat. He understood she wasn't the best at adult interactions and certain social situations, but he'd promised to give her a new experience every day—and today he was adding acceptable behavior towards your *secret* boyfriend in the school hallways.

He caught up just as she shut her staffroom door. Palming the door, he pushed it open before the lock clicked into place.

"What—?" Mad turned around. "Oh. It's you."

Stepping into the room, Toby closed the door behind him and leaned against it. With a quick scan, he saw they were the only ones in the English/History staffroom. Bringing his gaze back to Mad, he took her in. From the fugly black grandma shoes on her feet, the shapeless calf-length dark gray skirt and the equally formless cream blouse buttoned to her chin, to the scraped-back blonde curls ruthlessly pulled flat to her skull and confined in a bun on the back of her head.

His cock stirred.

God, she got him hot no matter what she wore. It probably didn't help that he knew what lay beneath that dowdy outfit. Or that he knew what she was willing to let him do to it. His cock was no longer stirred. It was well and truly shaken and standing at attention.

"You drive me absolutely mad, woman."

He lunged for her. Grabbed her wrist and dragged her against him. Ducking his head, he slanted his mouth over hers and thrust his tongue inside. He swallowed her squeak of protest whole.

Sweetness burst in his mouth. Her breath smelled sweet too. He couldn't place the flavor or scent and dove deeper for a better taste to try to figure it out. Slipping a hand to her nape, Toby tilted her head to the left, moved his to the right and fused their mouths completely.

Her fingers curled against his chest, her nails grazing one nipple and sending a shudder through him. Fuck. If he didn't slow down he'd have her on the floor, out of her clothes, with his cock rammed inside her in less than two minutes.

Easing back, he slowed the kiss and brought them down gently. Their lips clung as he withdrew completely and panted for breath. "Mad."

"I..." Her eyelids fluttered up and her unfocused gaze searched his. "Toby." She sighed his name.

He loved that he scrambled her brain enough to stop it. "Hey."

She smiled, her lips wet and trembling. "Hi."

"Now *that's* the tone I want to hear when I say 'hey' in the hall. Not that cold 'Mr. Moreland' shit you've been giving me."

"I...we can't let anyone find out..." She licked her lips and lowered her eyes. "I'm sorry. I don't know how to talk to you without it being obvious that we're seeing each other. We've already established I'm out of my element here."

"We have. And because I know you're struggling a little with this, I'm going to give you a hand. Tonight, we're going to practice you saying hi to me without sounding like you want to jump my bones." He grinned.

"Practice?"

"Yeah, I'm going to do all sorts of naughty things to you and you're going to practice talking in a normal voice while I do it."

Mad's mouth opened and closed. She shook her head. "That will never work."

"You're right. But it'll be fun trying." He waggled his eyebrows and scored a surprised laugh out of her. "We'll save the naughty things for after you perfect a neutral-toned 'Hi, Mr. Moreland' then."

The doorknob rattled at his back. Mad gasped and jumped back a good four feet. Toby simply turned around and opened the door as though he were on his way out.

"Oh." Melanie Hobbs put a hand to her chest. "You scared me."

"Hey. Sorry." He smiled and turned to look at Mad over his shoulder. "Thanks for your help."

Toby hustled out of there before Melanie could ask him any probing questions but he didn't miss the speculative look she swung between him and Madison. He kind of felt sorry for leaving Mad to deal with their nosey colleague, but it would be easier for her to deny their involvement if they weren't both in the same room.

He'd agreed to keep their relationship quiet but he wouldn't lie about it if asked, and he didn't think they'd be able to keep it a secret for long. Even if Mad mastered the art of a casual hello, the way Toby stripped her with his eyes whenever he laid them on her was a dead giveaway.

MADISON AIMED a strained smile at Melanie before darting to her desk and burying herself in grading papers. Since starting at Huntington College, she hadn't had more than a handful of conversations with the other woman but she didn't believe for one second that Melanie would let Toby's presence in their staffroom go without comment.

"So...what did Toby want?"

"Hmm..." Madison pretended to be distracted by what was on her desk. In truth, she couldn't focus on a single word. Glancing up, she tried to pull off a look of confusion and probably only succeed in looking constipated. "Sorry?"

"Toby Moreland. What did he want your help with?"

"Oh, a student." Best to stick to simple answers, less likely to get caught in a lie that way. Not that she was an expert on subterfuge.

"Which student?" Melanie pressed.

"Ah, I forget the boy's name, but it was about an English essay." Sounded plausible.

"Who's the boy's teacher? Shouldn't Toby have gone to the source for help?" Melanie continued to pepper her with question.

Madison bit her tongue to stop the truth from blurting out. Shaking her head, she looked down at the essay on her desk. It was one from a year-twelve student and it was intended to teach them how to apply for university. The perfect answer to Melanie's question formed in her head.

"It's not a class essay but one for a university application one of his player's needs to complete," Madison explained with a triumphant smile.

"Oh."

Madison could hear the disappointment in Melanie's voice. She had no idea what the other woman would be despondent about and honestly she didn't care, as long as the inquisition stopped.

Keeping their relationship a secret was going to be harder than Madison originally thought. She'd spent the last five days avoiding any possible chance of running into Toby because she couldn't guarantee she wouldn't smile at him in a way that would broadcast to all that they were having blazing-hot sex.

She couldn't stop the wanton thoughts from flashing through her brain whenever she brought Toby to mind; *seeing* him turned those imaginings down-right salacious. Add in her rapid pulse, shortened breath and dilated pupils, and anyone within fifty feet would know she was having sex with Toby in her head.

Madison wasn't sure whether to be thrilled that she appeared to be a normal red-blooded woman with a healthy sexual appetite, or appalled. She'd heard the term late-bloomer when referring to teenagers but what about a twenty-six-year-old woman?

"Hey, are you going to the game this afternoon?"

Madison's head snapped up. She'd totally forgotten Melanie was in the room with her. "The game?"

"Yeah, there's a footy game on the back field beginning fifth period. Some interschool thing. I don't know all the details but our guys are leading the comp, so Ted said if we wanted, we could take our classes out to watch and cheer our team on."

"Oh, well, I've got year-seven history last period..." Madison scrambled to remember what she'd planned for today's lesson. Research discussion. That could be put off until next week. "It probably wouldn't hurt for them to miss a lesson in the curriculum. There's plenty of time to make up the component."

"I've got year-eight English, and believe me, we could *all* do with sitting outside for one lesson." Melanie smiled as she gathered her things. "I'll see you there."

"Yes. See you then."

Madison let her forced smile drop when the door closed behind Melanie. If she were going to take her class to the game, she'd be seeing Toby again. She wasn't sure she could survive two sightings in one school day. And after that kiss...

Too late to back out now. If she didn't show up, Melanie would ask more questions and Madison had barely made it through this round. She'd have to try to seat her class as far away from Toby as possible.

Three hours later, Madison came to the conclusion that her luck had run out. Not only was the only space available for her class right behind were Toby stood at the bench for the school's team but Melanie and her class of year-eight students occupied the section next to her.

Madison had never watched a football game in her life. She had no clue what was going on and took her cues from her students and those around her, so she at least appeared to be encouraging and congratulating the team at the appropriate times.

At one point she even asked Mathew McKinney why the referee had blown the whistle, giving the other team the ball. After an extended, in-depth explanation, she was still none the wiser. And she considered herself a quick learner. Unfortunately, the rules of this game seemed beyond her.

The only thing she was sure of was the score. Huntington led 24-12.

When her eyes weren't glued to the game, they were glued to Toby. She's never seen him so serious. He called out to the players on the field and conferred with the ones on the bench, as well as the other teachers who appeared to hold positions within the team.

She recognized a few of the players too. They were all top students—and that thought brought her up short. She'd believed athletes were not the best students and therefore played sport. Madison had no idea how she'd drawn that conclusion when she couldn't recall ever learning the fact.

Had she done Toby a bigger injustice than she'd first thought?

Had she held some misconceived prejudice against him? Against all sportsmen?

The very thought shocked her. She'd considered herself a nonjudgmental person, each to their own and all that, but obviously she wasn't.

A whistle blew and the crowd around her erupted in cheers and applause. Glancing at the scoreboard, she noted the score remained 24-12 and Huntington retained their top position on the division ladder. Two minutes later, the end-of-school bell rang and she dismissed her class from the field instead of taking them back to the classroom.

Slipping her handbag strap over her shoulder, she turned and came face-to-face with Toby.

"Hey." He smiled down at her.

"H-hi." Okay, not quite a normal greeting but it was better than throwing her arms around his neck and crushing her mouth to his like she wanted to.

"How'd you like the game?"

"Um...it was good. We won."

Toby laughed. "And you have no clue what went on, do you?"

Smiling sheepishly, Madison said, "No. Even a detailed explanation from Mathew McKinney didn't help me."

"Don't worry, I'll teach you the rules sometime."

"Thanks. I'd like that. It was fun to watch and cheer, even if I didn't know what I was cheering for."

"Good. I'm glad. I promised the boys pizza if they won so I'll be here for a few more hours. Alright if I swing by your place later or do you want me to give you a key to mine?" Toby asked.

Madison was stunned by the offer of a key. She might not understand the full workings of a normal relationship but she was fairly certain that offering someone a key to your house was a significant step. "Ah..."

"And I see that I've thrown you completely with that question."

"No. It's just...a key? That's a big thing, right?"

He smiled. "Yes, it is."

"Right. Okay. Well, either option is suitable."

"Here." Toby grabbed her hand and pressed something into her palm before closing her fingers over it. "Do whatever you want with that. I'll text you when I leave here and we can decide what to do then."

"Okay."

"I really want to kiss you, Mad, but I won't. Just know that I want to." With a wink, he turned and walked away.

Glancing down, Madison opened her hand and saw the shiny silver key Toby had placed in her hand.

He'd given her a key to his house.

She'd been to the doctor's at the beginning of the week for the contraceptive pill and had already begun taking it.

She might be walking on unfamiliar territory but there was no denying they were treading on *Mount Serious*.

Smiling, she curled her fingers around Toby's key once more.

She'd file this in the 'new experience' box along with all the other things Toby had shown her in the last week.

God. Was it only a week since they'd returned from the history excursion? Seven days that felt like a lifetime. Seven days and she'd gone from being single, with no social life to speak of, to having a hot boyfriend who loved to indulge her in nights of pleasure—and not all of it in the bedroom, either.

This last week with Toby had been the best of her life. She couldn't wait to see what happened in the next one. Or the one after that. Or the one after. Or the one after...

17

TOBY HELD tight to Mad's hand. "It'll be fine. Stop worrying."

"It's a family dinner."

"I'm allowed to bring a date to a family dinner." He grinned at her but it didn't alleviate the frown lines from her beautiful face. Tugging her hand, he pulled her closer. "Come here."

Before she could protest, he kissed her. He breathed in her gasp and stroked his tongue over hers. She opened wider for him, let him taste and tease, and melted in his arms. Running his hands up and down her back, he soothed instead of inflamed. No point getting either of them worked up when they had to walk into his parents' house.

Letting her up for air, he trailed his lips to her ear. "New experience for today. We're together. That means we go to each other's family events. It's what couples do."

She shivered. "Oh."

God, he loved it when he kissed her and slowed that brain of hers. Nuzzling his nose under her jawline, he breathed her in. He could never get enough of her smell. Sweet and fresh with a lingering trace of the coconut water she liked to drink. "Hmm...you always smell like sugar..." He nipped at her chin. "And I've got such a sweet tooth."

"Get a room."

Toby turned. "You're just jealous I've got a pretty girl to kiss and you don't."

"Definitely."

Tucking Madison against his side, he faced his brother. "Mad, you remember my brother Damian."

"Ah, yes. Hi." Her face was flushed red, whether from embarrassment or arousal, he didn't know—possibly both.

"Hey there, pretty lady, when you've had enough of this douchebag, give me a call." Damian winked before sauntering up to the house.

"Ignore him." Toby tightened his arm around her. "He's a dick."

"Um..."

Toby laughed. "Sorry. Damian's a shit-stirrer. He's trying to get a rise out of me."

"And I got one," Damian called out.

"Damn." Toby sighed. "He did."

Before his brother could open the front door, it swung wide to reveal their mother. "Are you three finished playing in the yard?" she asked, her gaze bouncing between him and Damian.

"Damian's hitting on my girl," Toby complained.

"Damian Charles, find your own girl. And you," she pointed a finger at Toby, "keep your hands and lips to yourself for the next few hours."

If possible, Mad turned a shade redder and shrank into his side. Toby laughed. "Seriously, Mom, have you seen her? She's too hard to resist."

His mom smiled and went on her toes to kiss his cheek. "At least keep it G-rated."

Mad sucked in a breath and stiffened against him.

"Mom..."

"Sorry." She held out both her hands. "How are you, Madison? It's so good to see you again."

"N-nice to see you too."

Toby let his mother steal his date as they entered his childhood home. He could hear the rest of the family in the back of the house. They'd be congregated in the big room that opened out to the yard. It was the place they always hung out together. Now *and* when they were younger. Smiling, he followed two of his favorite women into the melee that was a Moreland family gathering.

"Hey, look who finally showed up," Cassie called from her seat where she nursed his nephew. "See there, baby boy, that's your uncle Damian and uncle Toby."

Walking over, Toby crouched and ran his hand over Bennett's soft head. "Is he eating?"

"No. Just finished. You want to hold him?"

"Yeah." Toby slipped his hands beneath the baby and pulled him against his chest. He couldn't get over how captivated he was by this little guy.

He'd been thinking about babies—kids—ever since his sister had delivered Bennett. When Mad had told him they were in the clear after their slip up, Toby had been disappointed in a way he never would have expected. He knew it wasn't the right time to be thinking about a family, but he couldn't help wondering what Mad would look like, her belly swollen with their child.

Humming softly, he rocked on his feet and snuggled the baby-powder-scented bundle against him. He could hear chatter around him but right now, the only thing he could focus on was Bennett.

Would he feel this much love with his own child? More?

Toby glanced over at Mad. She was busy talking to his mom and for once she didn't look like a deer caught in headlights. Laughing at something his mother said, she turned his way and smiled. He wanted to go to her, pull her into his arms and kiss her smiling mouth.

After her initial nervousness, she seemed to have settled. He'd keep an eye on her but he wanted her to do this on her own. She needed to know that she could talk to people without his help.

"She's different to your usual type." Cassie moved beside him, checked Bennett.

"Maybe." Toby didn't think she was that different. She was definitely more real. There was no falseness to her affections. None of the usual fawning behavior he seemed to inspire in women.

"She's not awed by you."

"What?" He turned to his sister.

"Madison isn't one of those bimbos looking for a free ride."

"Is that what you think of the women I've dated?"

Cassie laughed. "I've only ever known you to date one girl, and that was back in high school, the rest you just fucked."

"Hey." He tried to cover Bennett's little ears.

"Ha. That boy heard more this morning when I *still* couldn't get my jeans to do up."

"It's been a week. I'm pretty sure you're not supposed to fit back into them yet."

"Sue me for trying." She reached out for the baby. "Let me take him. I'm going to put him in the nursery so Mommy can have some adult time."

"Stir crazy already?" He handed Bennett to his sister.

"No. But if I don't make myself put him down, I never will. He's too precious for words." Cassie cuddled Bennett close, nuzzled his cheek with her nose.

"He is," Toby agreed as he watched his sister loving on her son.

When she walked away, Damian stepped up with a beer in each hand. "Thought you'd like a drink."

"Thanks."

"I like her," his brother said, tipping his bottle in Mad's direction.

"You made that clear outside."

"Yeah, well, that was a joke, this isn't. You're different with her."

"How?" He tilted his head and studied Damian.

"I don't know. I can't work out what it is exactly." Damian shrugged.

Toby laughed. "Well that's enlightening. Thanks."

Damian grinned. "No worries. Glad I could help."

He shook his head. "I think this is the weirdest conversation we've had, big brother, and I'm including the 'talk' about safe sex you felt it your duty to give me."

"Hey, someone had to be sure your pecker didn't get you in trouble with all those women."

"I was twenty. My pecker was well versed in the ways of women by then."

Damian laughed. "God, you probably got lucky before I did."

"Ah, no, you definitely got lucky first."

Eyeing him skeptically, Damian mumbled, "You sound pretty sure about that."

"Bindi Arnold. You were a week past your sixteenth birthday."

Damian choked on his beer. "What?" he spluttered.

Toby smiled. "The walls in this house are thin."

"Jesus Christ."

Toby laughed. "Yeah, I recall her calling out for god's help."

"Shut up," Damian growled before walking away.

MADISON TOOK the top card and read the words.

Movie: Magic Mike

Okay. That shouldn't be too hard. Turning to the board, she lifted the marker and drew a magician's hat.

"Hat," Toby called out.

She kept drawing, adding a rabbit.

"Mad Hatter."

Glaring at Toby, she pointed to the hat.

"Hat?"

"Oh, I know!" Cassie jumped to her feet.

"You're not on their team, Cass." Luc grabbed his wife's wrist and pulled her back down beside him.

"But I know what it is," she whined.

Turning back to the board, Madison added a wand to the picture. She tilted her head and squinted. They were quite good renditions, considering she wasn't all that artistic.

"Rabbit. Hat. Stick."

Stick? Glaring at Toby again, she decided to try the second part of the movie title. So far he hadn't guessed one of her drawings and she'd guess every one of his. And he couldn't draw to save his life.

The timer ticked down and while she might have done all right with objects and the occasional animal, drawing a man was a completely different—and impossible—achievement.

Standing back, she eyed the stick figure and burst out laughing.

"Hey, no talking!" Damian called out.

"Is that R2D2?" Toby asked.

"Oh god." Cassie buried her face in her hands.

The buzzer sounded.

"It's Magic Mike, you idiot!" Cassie tossed a pillow at Toby.

"Really? I don't see it..."

Madison threw up her hands. "I give up. You suck."

Toby arched one eyebrow, and one side of his mouth kicked up to match. "Oh really?"

"Gotta admit, brother, she's right. You guys are in the lead only because Madison has gotten every one of your pictures correct," Adam said after consulting the point sheet.

"She should have gotten a handicap being paired with you. Not that she needs it."

Madison smiled at Toby's sister. "Thank you."

"You know if we played girls versus boys, we'd still kick their asses and there's more of them than us," Cassie added.

"Don't even think about it, Cassandra Maree," Mrs. Moreland called out from the kitchen, where she and Mr. Moreland were enjoying some quality time with their grandson.

"Ah, c'mon, mom. I gotta get my thrills somewhere."

"You are not wiping the floor with those boys tonight," Mrs. Moreland replied.

"So you agree we'd win?" Cassie grinned.

"Come and get your boy. He's hungry again."

"My god. That kid is going on the bottle." Cassie stood and headed for the kitchen. "I swear it feels like he's permanently attached to my boob."

"At least someone's getting boob around here," Adam muttered.

"He's not the only one," Toby murmured, his hot gaze on Madison.

Fire burst low and deep, heat rushed over her skin, leaving a prickly trail that had goose bumps popping up and her breath stuttering. "Toby!" His name exploded from her throat on a gasp of air.

He grinned.

"At the risk of repeating myself...get a room," Damian said as he rose from his spot on the floor. "And on that note, I'm out of here. Catch you all later."

"Yeah, we're gonna head out too." Toby stood, held out his hand. "Ready, Mad?"

Ready? Her blood was thrumming, her heart was pounding and the crotch of her undies was wet. Oh yeah, she was ready. And thoroughly mortified to be in this condition at his parents' house.

"I'll say goodbye to your parents." Without making eye contact with any of the remaining people in the room, she strode towards the kitchen.

Hopefully by the time she arrived in front of Toby's parents, she wouldn't look like a berry about to burst. And if not, that they at least didn't work out that she was thinking about doing very inappropriate things to their son.

18

A SMILE TUGGED at Toby's mouth as he pulled his car in beside Mad's. Taking a moment, he just sat there staring at her little compact parked in his driveway. The sight shouldn't make him this happy but there was no denying the elation that arced through him.

This was the first time she'd come over to his house and used the key he'd given her. Every other visit she'd perfectly coincided with his arrival, so she wouldn't have to be in his house without him. He'd pushed her the last few days and finally, he'd gotten what he wanted.

He was going to open his front door and come home to Mad.

Damn, that totally made up for his shitty day. Pocketing his keys, Toby got out of the car and walked up the path. Before he reached the door, it opened wide and there she was, all smiles and happy-to-see-him eyes.

His heart pounded in his chest, his body tightened from head to toe and a thrum of anticipation shot through his veins.

"Hi." Mad's smile slipped. "What's wrong?"

Toby arched an eyebrow. "What makes you think something's wrong?"

She reached up and brushed a finger beside his mouth, then grazed it over the skin at the corner of his left eye. "Your mouth is drawn and your eyes are crinkled at the edges, the way they do when you're concerned or distressed about something."

He pulled her into his arms and held her close. "You know all that about me?"

"Of course," she murmured against his chest, her arms circling his waist. "I'm used to studying things, remember. And lately you're my favorite subject."

"Hmm..." The idea of being her favorite anything pleased him. "We lost. The other team took some dirty shots, hurt three of our top players doing so, and we won't know for a few days how serious those injuries are."

Mad leaned back in his arms. "Oh, I'm sorry. The boys must be disappointed."

"No more so than me."

"Come inside. I'll get you a beer and something to eat."

"Sounds good." He dropped a kiss on her forehead. She smelled of spices and garlic.

"We could cancel tonight if you're not up to it," she offered.

"No." He turned them and guided her into the house. "Definitely not. This is another new experience, and you get the bonus of a moody boyfriend thrown in."

"Only if you're sure. I don't mind."

"Mad, how much fun have you had getting everything ready for tonight?"

She ducked her head. "A little bit."

Toby laughed. "That's an outright lie. You've Googled recipes and ingredients and spent hours on YouTube glued to demonstration videos. I *know* you're excited about tonight. Plus everyone will kill me if we cancel this late."

Her smile was blinding. "Okay. And you're right. Until this week, I never realized how much I *love* cooking. I mean, I knew I could cook, and enjoyed it, but preparing a meal for only myself is completely different from organizing and making one for fourteen people."

Excitement sparkled in her eyes and she practically bounced on her toes with suppressed energy. He couldn't resist kissing her. She tasted sweet and spicy. There was a hint of garlic, possibly cream...

"Hmm...you taste good." Diving back in, Toby thrust his tongue against hers to find more of the flavors she'd been sampling while making a meal for his family.

He palmed her ass and brought her to her toes. Moaning into his mouth, Mad rubbed herself against him. Toby went from horny to desperate in a heartbeat. It didn't matter how many times he had her, the thrill that ran though him whenever he got his hands on her sliced him to the bone.

"Do we have time for a quickie?" he growled as he rocked his hard cock into her soft center.

"You're never satisfied with quick." She nibbled along his jaw up to his ear, tugged on the lobe. "We've got thirty minutes until the timer goes off on the oven."

Toby grinned. "Bet I can get you off in half that. Twice."

Mad laughed. "That's a sucker's bet. I'm not taking it." She pushed out of his arms. "Race you."

He stood gaping as she darted away from him and headed for the master bedroom.

This wasn't the same woman he'd started seeing four weeks ago. She'd come out of her shell, and the more she revealed, the more Toby wanted to see.

He'd spent every day of those four weeks showing her what

she'd missed. He grinned when he thought about the night they'd made out in the back of the movie cinema. The water fight he'd disguised as washing their cars. Riding the ferry over to the zoo. Toby had to admit, he'd had as much fun seeing Mad enthralled with each new adventure as she'd had experiencing them.

"Hey! I thought you wanted a quickie?" A pair of Mad's sexy underwear flew out his bedroom door and fluttered to the floor not five meters away.

Toby grinned. Oh yeah, definitely not the same woman.

MADISON HUMMED as she arranged the fruit she'd sliced earlier around the base of the Pavlova she'd made from scratch. For a first attempt, it didn't look half bad.

"Can I help with something?" Toby's mom asked as she came into the kitchen with a tray of dirty dishes.

"Oh. No." Madison quickly met her. "Let me take those."

"Nonsense. You continue putting that yummy-looking dessert together. I can load these in the dishwasher."

"Toby should—"

"I asked him not to."

She stared at Mrs. Moreland. "Oh."

The older woman smiled sweetly but it didn't stop Madison's stomach from summersaulting.

Swallowing through her constricted throat, Madison asked, "Is this where you tell me I'm not good enough for your son?"

"What?" Mrs. Moreland put the tray on the counter and turned to face Madison. "No. Why would you think that? Never mind. What I have to say is the complete opposite."

Madison could only stare.

"You are the best thing to ever come into my son's life."

"Mrs.—"

Toby's mom held up a hand. "First, it's Lisa. Second, let me finish before you argue with me. Can you do that for me?"

Again, Madison remained mute. Just nodded like a bobble-head doll on a car dashboard.

"Good." Talking a deep breath, Lisa settled her gaze on Madison's. "Tobias has had some amazing things happen to him. He's represented the country in his chosen sport and made a better-than-average living from the same sport. My boy's been lucky. And I don't care what anyone says, the injury that sidelined him did not end his good fortune.

"He's thrived teaching. Every one of those kids he's guided has been lucky to have him, but he's also lucky to have *them*. He's doing what he was born to do, regardless of what the sports commentators say about the waste of good talent. But you? God, I've watched him...heard him since he met you. He's better than he was. He was always great but for *you*, he's amazing."

"I—"

"You said you'd let me finish," Lisa said with a smile.

"Sorry."

She cupped Madison's cheeks in her small warm hands. "He's told me quite a bit about you. I know all about where you've come from, and seeing you now, you're better too. Together, you're better. That's something to hold on to."

Madison nodded. She couldn't think of anything to say and she feared anything she *did* say would disappoint Lisa. In the short time she'd come to know Toby's mother, Madison had grown to respect and admire the woman. She'd raised an amazing family with unconditional love and wasn't shy of telling them if they were out of line even now, with all of them adults.

No. Madison definitely didn't want to disappoint Toby's mother.

Lightly patting Madison's cheeks, Lisa said, "You think on that. I'm going back out with the family."

Before this conversation, Madison had known what she and Toby had was special. At first she'd believed it had to do with him being the only guy to give her sexual pleasure, but it had soon become obvious to her that sex wasn't all they had between them.

She had no idea how Toby felt. If his affection went as deep as Madison feared hers did. Having never been in love, she couldn't be sure, except the thought of being without Toby... Her stomach cramped, her chest ached, constricted, making it hard to breathe.

Was this what love felt like?

And if it was, what should she do about it? Tell him?

It didn't seem prudent to do so when she wasn't certain.

"Hey, everything okay in here?" Toby walked up behind her and slipped his arms around her waist. "That dessert ready yet? I'm dying to try it."

Plastering on a smile and scrubbing her mind clear of her jumbled thoughts, she turned her head and pressed a kiss to his jaw. "Almost. Want to grab plates and cutlery for me?"

"Sure." He let her go and spun her around. "But first, I want some of my favorite kind of sugar."

His mouth came down on hers and she opened. Melting into the kiss—into him—Madison sank into the pleasure zipping through her veins. Toby's kisses always set her on fire. The way he swept his tongue into her mouth, the way he demanded while giving her everything, it sizzled and fizzed and consumed.

He broke away. "Wow. Okay. Hold that thought. We'll get back to that after everyone leaves."

She smiled. Her face was flushed and she was certain if she went outside right now, everyone would know what her and Toby had been doing. "I need to finish the dessert." Sticking her head in the refrigerator for a few minutes to get the whipped cream should cool her down.

Stepping away from Toby's heat, she opened the fridge door and stood in the cool air wafting out of the opening.

Toby moved in beside her. "I could do with a bit of cooling off myself." He glanced down.

Madison followed his gaze to the erection tenting his pants. A giggle escaped her.

"I'm not finding this funny." Toby rearranged himself. "I can't go out there and face my mother like this."

"The advantage of being a female."

"Really?" He arched an eyebrow and directed his stare to her chest. "Because..."

Looking down, Madison saw her nipples were hard and attempting to poke holes in her top. "Oh god." She slapped her hands over them.

Laughing, Toby pulled her into his arms. "Have I told you how much I love your tits?"

"Only every time you get your hands or mouth on them." She shivered, thinking about the stroke of his hands, the wet heat of his mouth.

"I'm not sure you appreciate my devotion. I think I'll have to remedy that later." He squeezed her ass, lifting her to her toes. "And your ass. I'm really, *really* devoted to your ass."

Madison moaned and dropped her forehead to his shoulder. "Stop. We'll never be able to go back outside at this rate."

"If we don't return, do you think they'll just go home?"

"No." She shoved him away. "Get the plates and cutlery."

Smiling, he gave her a love tap on the ass as he passed her to do her bidding.

She trembled from head to toe, and even after standing in the open fridge door and sucking in several deep breaths of cold air, her nerves were so jangled she could only think of one thing.

Toby spending the rest of the night showing her his appreciation.

19

TOBY CRANED his neck and lifted his ass out of the seat to see over the crowd.

"Who the hell are you looking for?"

He swiveled back to face Adam. "No one."

On the other side of Adam, Cooper laughed. "Did you invite Madison?"

He lasered a dark look his younger brother's way.

"Jesus. You're in love with her," Coop said with a shake of his head.

Love? He wanted to fuck her ten ways to Sunday every damn day and couldn't stand it when they weren't together, but love... He wasn't in love with Mad. Was he?

"My god you're idiot. Coop's right." Damian leaned forward in his seat. "You're totally in love with Madison."

"What the hell would Coop know?" Toby grumbled.

Adam laughed. "I'd think him and Zac were the experts on that subject, so if he says you're in love with her then you are. What say you, Zac?"

Zac studied him from where he sat on the other end of their

brotherly row. "Yep. Totally know the signs. And they're flashing neon red right across your forehead, big brother."

What the fuck? Why was his love life suddenly to topic of conversation? "What the hell did you put in the beers, Damian?"

All his brothers laughed at him and Toby was on the verge of punching the closest one when Cooper tipped his chin, indicating something behind Toby.

"Here comes the love of your life now," Damian added.

Whirling around in his seat, Toby watched Mad make her way down the aisle towards their row. She'd worn blue jeans and a jumper in a deep green that set off her creamy skin and blonde hair. The sweeping curls—left down, the way he like them—moved around her shoulders, played peek-a-boo with her tits and had his palms itching to tangle his fingers through the strands he knew from experience were silky soft.

Holy shit!

It slammed him like a front-row forward.

He was positively one hundred percent completely in love with Madison Keibler.

"There ya go. Now you get it," Coop said behind him.

"Fuck. What the hell do I do now?" he asked, a little in awe of the emotion filling him.

"Make sure she doesn't get away, dumb fuck." This sage wisdom came from his oldest brother.

"How?" Toby mumbled.

"Shit. If I knew that, I wouldn't be spending most weekends screwing nameless women at the club," Damian answered.

Toby didn't have the time or the brainpower to work out that little nugget of info from his oldest brother. Right now, all he could think about was how to make Mad his.

Permanently.

He smiled, the stretch of his lips growing wider the closer she came. Politely excusing herself from the two men on the end of their row, she turned side-on and shuffled past them to the empty seat beside Toby.

"Hi." She leaned in and kissed him.

He was too stunned by his epiphany to return her kiss, and she'd taken her seat before Toby realized he wanted more. Grabbing her hand, he wove his fingers through hers and settled their joined hands on his leg. "Do you want a drink?"

"I'm good at the moment." She leaned forward and looked past him at his brothers. "Hi guys."

He ignored them and concentrated on Mad. "Ready to see a professional game live?"

"Yes. What game are we watching?"

"Dogs versus Dragons," Adam answered.

"I got that from all the supporters on the way in, but what game is it?" Mad sat on the edge of her seat and peered down at the field.

"Umm..." Adam glanced at him and shrugged. "Round six."

Toby chuckled. He knew what she was asking.

"No. What *game*? Soccer, Union, League, AFL— what game?"

Adam's mouth dropped open. "You don't know what *type* of game we're watching?"

"Toby just said it was a footy game." She shrugged. "I've never been into sport so I don't know a football from a soccer ball."

"Well first, it's League, and second, Soccer is not footy." Adam punched Toby in the arm. "How could you let this woman's lack of footy knowledge go on for so long? Move over. I'll teach her."

"Not a chance, big brother." Toby turned his back on Adam

and with two fingers under Mad's chin, brought her gaze to his. "You ready for a crash course?"

"Yes. So this is the code you used to play, right?"

"Yep. The St. George Dragons are my old team."

"Really? Is that the team you go for then?"

"I'm partial to them but growing up, we were Roosters supporters. Dad still goes to all their home games."

"So we're going for the Dragons?"

"Yes."

"Are they good?"

"Their season has started off all right. Too early to tell if they'll make finals but on paper they're good, and they've performed well in their games so far," Toby explained.

"Is this the same code as the school team played the other week?" Mad chewed her bottom lip. "I really should have Googled the rules."

"No. That was Union. I'll give you the basics and explain anything more in-depth as it comes up in play. How's that sound?"

"All right. Go."

Toby barely got the list of players' positions out before Mad's eyes started to glaze over. She might be a genius who skipped grades, but it appeared the rules of League were beyond her. "How about we just watch? It might be easier to point out the rules as they happen."

"Yes, that might be best. It *is* a little confusing. All those people on the field at once..."

Beside him, Adam chuckle behind his beer. "I can't believe you're dating a girl who hasn't a clue about the sport you live and breathe for," his brother muttered.

Turning to his brother, Toby smiled. "I know. But I *don't* live and breathe for the sport. Never did."

It might have looked that way to others, but Toby had

always known he'd be a teacher. He just happened to be good at football and like most things he did, he did them to succeed. And until he'd blown out his knee, he'd been at the top of the game.

~

"HEY!" Madison jumped to her feet. "He can't do that!" Spinning to look at Toby, she asked, "Can he?"

"No." He shook his head. "It was a cheap shot because they're losing and frustrated, plus time is ticking down."

Dropping back into her seat again, she glanced at the huge scoreboard at the end of the field. "Three minutes left?"

"Yep." Toby patted her leg. "Don't worry. We've got this."

He meant the Dragons, but since the first whistle blew it had been 'we'. As though being a spectator made you one of the team. She'd really enjoyed the atmosphere of the game. Liked being among a large group of people wanting the same outcome. It was strange but thrilling to sit here in the middle of it—to be a part of it.

For the next few minutes she sat on the edge of her seat, counting down the seconds. Toby and his brothers did the same, and when the final siren blasted through the stadium, Madison jumped to her feet with all the other Dragons supporters and cheered.

Throwing herself into Toby's arms, she gave him a smacking kiss. "Thanks for inviting me."

"I take it you had fun then?" he asked with a mischievous twinkle in his eyes.

She grinned. "Maybe a little bit."

"Good. Another new experience for you."

"One I want to do again. When's the next game?"

"They play every week," Adam leaned in to say. "And

thank you, Madison, for making today's game more exciting than usual."

"I did?"

"Your enthusiasm, regardless of your cluelessness, was fun to watch."

"Wait. I think that's a backhanded compliment..." Madison glared at Toby's brother.

Adam laughed. "Not what I intended. Are you joining us for dinner?"

"Oh, you're all going to dinner?"

"That was the plan, but if you don't want to go, we don't have to," Toby said.

"You go. Have dinner with your brothers. I'll go home." She didn't want to intrude on their male bonding time. Within ten minutes of arriving at the game, she'd worked out that's what this day was about for them.

"Ah, let's see...go home with you, smelling all sweet and warm, or go have dinner with my beer-smelling, ugly-mugged brothers...? No contest. You win hands down." Toby wrapped an arm around her waist.

"Do we get that option?" Damian asked.

"Nope." Toby slid his other arm around her and picked her up. "She's all mine. Get your own."

Madison squealed when he started to walk away, carrying her. "Put me down."

"No. Can't risk one of them stealing you."

She laughed. "No chance of that happening."

Serious eyes met hers. "Promise?"

Madison wasn't sure what to make of Toby's sudden mood switch. But it was easy to give him what he'd asked for though. "Promise."

"Good. Let's get out of here."

"If you put me down we could do that quicker."

"But I like you in my arms."

"I know, and I promise to let you carry me again when we get home."

His eyes dilated, the pupils expanding to swallow up the dark brown. "Will you be naked," he whispered.

A shiver went through her. "If that's what you want."

"Oh, I want. I want and want and want. It's my permanent state with you."

"That sounds serious."

"It is."

Madison's insides clenched. What were they talking about? Sometimes she still found it hard to decipher those between-the-lines sentiments. She'd improved over the weeks she'd been with Toby, but every now and then she tripped up.

Before she could probe deeper, his brothers surrounded them.

"Put her down, Toby. Security is looking this way, and I don't like the way that rent-a-cop has his hand on...what the hell is that?" Damian leaned around Madison to get a closer look. "Jesus. It's a flashlight. Never mind, if he comes this way we can take him."

"Please tell me you do not have your gun on you," Coop growled.

"Hell no. I'd never get that through the security check at the gate. It's in the car."

Toby shook his head. "Damian. Go away. All of you. Go. Away."

Laughing, the four of them clapped Toby on the shoulder and said goodbye. Watching them go over her own shoulder, Madison waited until they were all out of sight to face Toby again.

"You can put me down now. The threat has gone."

"That one has." He started walking again. "Gotta protect what's mine."

Madison sucked in a breath as those words slid through her.

What's mine.

If she didn't know before those two words, she did now.

She was in love Tobias Moreland—and she had no idea how to tell him.

20

TOBY WEAVED his way through the milling students as he headed to Mad's classroom. He needed to grab a quick word to let her know he was going with Jim Landry and his mother to the specialist to find out if the kid would play again this season or at all.

Jim was a nervous wreck and his mother was no help; she'd almost hyperventilated in Toby's office. No wonder Jim asked him to accompany them this afternoon.

"Sir. Sir."

Toby turned to see Andy Sturgis jogging his way. "Hey, Andy, what's up? I'm in a bit of a hurry."

"Have you heard any more about Jim's knee? Is he out for the rest of the year?"

They both knew if the injury was as bad as feared, Jim would more than likely be out for longer than one season. The type of damage the promising five-eighth had sustained was career-ending. Toby ought to know. It was the injury that had ended his NRL career.

He tried for a reassuring smile. "We won't know anything

definite until he sees the specialist. I'll let Jim know you were asking and tell him to call you."

"Okay. Thanks."

"Sure." Toby was about to turn away when he remembered Jim wasn't the only one with injury concerns. "Hey, how's that thigh doing?"

"Good. No pain or stiffness. The physio gave me the all clear to play again."

"Excellent. We'll see you at training then."

Returning to his original trajectory, Toby put enough purpose in his stride to cut a clear path through the throng and an expression on his face that said *don't talk to me*. He wouldn't normally begrudge any student stopping him to say hi or ask a question but he needed to get to Mad before her next class started.

He spotted her entering her room and knew he had about a minute to get in and get out without drawing attention to them. She still insisted they keep their relationship on the quiet here at work and for now he'd respect that, but from where he stood, things were getting serious and he planned on bringing that subject up with her very soon.

"Hey." Toby entered the room and did a quick scan for anyone else. They were alone.

"Oh, Toby." Her gaze darted to the door behind him. "What are you doing in here?"

"Quickly. I need to tell you I won't be at home this afternoon. I'm going with Jim Landry to his specialist appointment to find out the results on his knee injury."

"Okay."

"I'll ring you as soon as I'm done. I've got Mal covering training so I'll be home right after I finish up with Jim."

"Sure. Not a problem."

He didn't think—it was second nature now whenever they were together. He leaned in and dropped a kiss on her mouth.

The gasp and the 'oh my god' behind him sent a jolt of alarm through his blood. Fuck.

Before he could suck in a breath, Mad jerked away from him. It didn't take a genius to work out what was going through her head right now.

Shit. Why hadn't they discussed the stupid clause in her contract before now? He didn't have the same one as Mad, his only mentioned teacher/student fraternization, not teacher/teacher.

"It's okay," he whispered so as not to be overheard.

She shook her head.

"Mad."

"Go. Just go." Her voice was tight and low, barely heard over the pounding of his own heart.

"Mad—"

"Go." This time the word was propelled at him like an arrow.

"We'll talk later."

She shook her head.

He didn't have the option of arguing further; the bell rang and he knew they'd be surrounded by students in seconds.

Turning away, he left Mad to whatever doom and gloom thoughts she was having, glared daggers at the two girls standing just inside the door and mentally yelled every swear word he knew. In the hall, students swamped him as they rushed to get to class.

Fucking hell. Of all the times for them to get caught together, it had to be now, when he couldn't take the time to soothe Mad's concerns. By the time he could, she'd have worked herself into a right state. He'd seen it in her eyes.

She was freaking out.

And Toby had a gut feeling that it wasn't going to be easy to overcome.

~

MADISON PUSHED into the staffroom and rushed to her desk. She tried to gather her things quickly so she could get out before anyone else came in. The last thing she wanted to deal with were looks and questions from her colleagues. It was bad enough dealing with them from her students.

As much as she'd hoped she'd thwarted any gossip about her and Toby, she hadn't. By the time the last class of the day rolled around, they were the talk of the school. Rumors abounded. So far she hadn't heard one version of the truth. Most were exaggerated to the nth degree.

One even had them fucking on her desk, for god's sake. Who would believe that? Then again, she was referring to a group of hormone-driven adolescents, so perhaps their fabricated stories weren't that surprising.

Slinging her handbag over her shoulder, she picked up the box of year-seven history assignments that she planned to mark this evening. Hopefully she'd be able to focus on doing her job and not on whether or not she'd lose that job come morning.

She was surprised to make it all the way to the parking lot before anyone stopped her. Unfortunately, she couldn't ignore Principal Richardson. The glower on his face didn't bode well.

"Mr. Richardson."

"Madison. I believe we have a problem."

"Yes, Sir."

"Want to tell me why I'm hearing about you and Toby Moreland in the hallways?"

"What's being said isn't the truth."

"And what is?"

Madison swallowed. "We're seeing each other."

"How long?"

"A few weeks now."

"Right. Well. I'm afraid we have a *real* problem then. Your contract with this school states no fraternizing with staff or students."

Oh god.

Her stomach dropped. Bile rose in her throat. She'd never checked. She'd meant to but she'd been so wrapped up in Toby that she'd forgotten all about her concern. Now she was going to be terminated because of it. They probably both were.

"You understand I have to take this to the board members? There will be a full investigation and both of you will more than likely be put on leave without pay until the matter is resolved."

"Yes, sir." She was numb. Could no longer feel her fingers or toes.

"Can you be in my office at eight tomorrow morning?"

Madison nodded. It appeared her vocal cords had gone numb too.

"I'll see you then." He smiled grimly. "Goodnight."

She didn't say anything. *Couldn't* say anything. It wasn't until Mr. Richardson was out of sight that Madison snapped out of her frozen state and rushed to her car.

The last person she wanted to deal with right now leaned against the driver's door.

Toby.

Quickening her pace, she stopped a few feet away so as not to give anyone who might see them the wrong idea. "You shouldn't be here."

He straightened to his full height. "Why the hell not?"

"Because I was right. There's a clause in my employment

contract. I would think in yours too. Our situation is being taken to the board members."

"I'm not worried about the board."

"Well I am. We could lose our jobs."

"I don't give a shit about that."

"*I* do." Her voice rose with every word she spoke and she tried to bring it back down, get it under control, get a grip on the panic exploding inside her. She'd never done anything remotely wrong in her life and now she'd blatantly ignored a legally binding contract to the point she could lose her job. Toby could lose *his*.

"Mad." He stepped towards her and she dodged to the side.

Hitting the button on her key to unlock the car, she yanked the rear passenger door open and put her things on the back-seat. Slamming the door, she faced Toby. "Get out of my way."

"Mad."

"No. I can't do this now. I have assignments to mark and a meeting in the principal's office at eight tomorrow. I can't deal with you too." Her chin wobbled, her eyes stung. She sucked in a breath and bit the inside of her cheek. She refused to cry in front of him.

"Madison, please. Talk to me."

"Not now. I need to go."

She didn't fool herself into thinking she had the strength to push Toby out of her way. He moved because he wanted to. Regardless, she opened her door, slid into the driver's seat and closed herself in the stuffy interior.

Refusing to look at Toby, she started the car and reversed out of her spot. She didn't even look at him in the rearview mirror as she drove away.

But she wanted to.

21

TOBY STOOD in the principal's office listening to the bullshit flowing out of Ted's mouth. He clenched his jaw and hands. So far he hadn't heard anything that wasn't the board trying to cover their asses with regard to teacher-student inappropriate behavior. He'd read the clause in his contract last night. Even called his mate, Brett, to get his take on the clause.

As a lawyer, Brett had been able to tell him that the clause was a standard one and any lawyer with a brain could work around it, and to let him know what happened after today's meeting. Toby was beginning to think he no longer wanted to work for a school with such a crappy attitude towards their staff.

He could certainly understand the board needed a position on staff interaction, but he and Mad hadn't done anything to compromise the school, corrupt the students or let their relationship affect their work.

Ted was blowing a lot of hot air—and Toby was done listening.

Until he mentioned Mad, specifically. Then he was all ears.

"As per school policy, Madison, and due to your disclosure of your relationship with Toby, the board feels it best to terminate your contract at this—"

Toby slammed his fists on the desk. "Fuck policy!"

Ted jumped. Mad gasped.

"Toby! I signed a contract."

"Fuck the contract, too." He grabbed a bundle of Post-it notes off Ted's desk, snatched up a pen, and began writing.

"W-what are you doing?" Mad asked.

"Handing in my resignation."

"What? No, Toby, you can't! The school needs you."

"Well I don't need *them*. Especially when some pompous ass is going to sit in a boardroom and tell me who I can and can't love! Fuck that bullshit." He scribbled his signature and threw the whole stack of notes at Ted. "There. It's done."

He spun on his heel and left before he completely blew his top and tore Ted's office to shreds.

"Toby, please..." Mad ran behind him.

Stopping, he sucked in a deep breath and turned to face her. "This is the best way. I don't need the job, Mad. I don't actually need to work another day in my life."

"What?"

"I'm loaded. Never spent any of the money I earned playing footy except to build the house, and Adam's had his hands on the rest of it from day one. He's more than quadrupled my nest egg."

"But—"

He placed a finger over her mouth. "My job is the *least* I'd give up for you." Taking his finger from her mouth, he dragged the tip across her cheek. "Don't you get it yet, Mad? I'd give up everything for you."

Bending down, he placed his lips on her forehead. He

didn't dare kiss her on the mouth. Pulling back, he laid his brow on hers.

"I love you. This definitely isn't the time or place I wanted to reveal that, but never let it be said that I can't roll with what life throws at me. I don't want to be the reason you lose this job."

"Toby." Her warm breath fanned his face and he closed his eyes for a moment.

"Madison. Please, let me do this for you." He cupped her cheek and swallowed the ball of emotion stuck in his throat. "For once in your life, let someone else put you first. Let *me* put you first."

As much as he wanted to hash this out now, he knew he had to leave. Straightening, he took a step back. With a half smile curling his mouth, Toby turned and walked away.

I'D GIVE up everything for you.

I love you.

Let me put you first.

Toby's words kept spinning around in her head. She hadn't seen or heard from him in three days and she hadn't been brave enough to seek him out.

The doorbell rang and her heart leapt.

Toby.

Except it wasn't Toby.

Opening the door, Madison greeted the woman on the other side. "Mrs. Moreland."

"I thought we'd established it was Lisa?" she asked as she brushed past Madison and into the house.

"I'm not sure—"

"Close the door and come inside."

Meekly, Madison did as she was told. What was it about the Morelands that had her jumping to obey?

"You look like shit. Let's sit down so you don't fall at my feet." Lisa grabbed Madison's hand and towed her into the living room. "Honestly, you two are as bad as each other."

"Mrs...Lisa. I'm not sure what—"

"Everything. Tobias told me everything. Now *you* tell me."

"I—"

"Sit. I'll make coffee then we'll talk."

"Let me—"

"Madison."

Tears stung her eyes and the back of her throat, her nasal passages. She'd never had the 'mother voice' used on her before. Madison's mother never reprimanded her because she'd never gone against instruction. She'd been the perfect little student, and now she was being treated like a daughter.

Blinking rapidly, Madison waved a hand in front of her face. "Sorry."

"Oh sweetie, there's no need to be sorry."

"But I hurt Toby." A sob choked off her words.

"Honey, he's not hurt by you. He's hurting *for* you."

"I don't understand."

"My son knows you all too well, I think. He knows you're sitting here feeling guilty and responsible for everything that happened. Especially about him quitting his job."

"He shouldn't have done that."

"Madison, if either of you had read that clause in your contract before your relationship was discovered, he'd have quit. And he'd have done it without a second thought."

"Why?"

"Because that's what we do for the people we love."

"But he's worked there for years."

"That's neither here nor there. What's important is for you

to realize that you didn't *cost* him anything. He *willing* gave it up for you."

"I don't understand that kind of sacrifice."

"All you have to know is that to him, it's not a sacrifice. It's a pleasure. His only desire is to give you what you want and need, what makes you happy. For Tobias, that was walking away from his job so you could keep yours."

"He walked away from me too," Madison whispered.

Lisa laughed. "No he didn't."

"He hasn't contacted me or tried to see me in days."

"He's giving you time to work out all that business at school. He wants that all sorted out before the two of you sit down to discuss the two of you. But as a mother who's seen her share of heartbroken people, I knew you'd need a little kick to get you moving. Although unlike my son, you appear to have showered in the last three days..."

Madison shot to her feet. "He can't come here. Toby can't come to me."

"Oh? Why ever not?" Lisa asked with a smile.

"Because he's always coming to me. Every step of the way he's come to me. Pushed me. I need to meet him halfway or he won't know."

"Know what dear?" Lisa prompted

"That I love him as much as he loves me. That I'd give up everything for him too. Well, except he won't let me because he's a caveman in disguise most of the time. But I have to show him I'm in this one hundred percent."

"There you go. I knew you'd get there quickly."

Madison looked around for her bag. Where did she put her keys?

"I'll leave you to it then." With a little wave, Toby's mother let herself out.

Staring at the closed door, Madison wondered what kind of

superpowers that woman had. Both times they'd had a serious conversation, Lisa had said very little, and yet on both occasions the results were monumental for Madison. She felt changed inside each time Lisa spoke to her.

Where the hell were her keys and purse?

22

TOBY LEANED FORWARD and lowered his head into his hands.

Three days.

Seventy-two hours.

A lifetime.

Fuck, he missed her. Like a leg or an arm, Mad's absence ached with a numbness that sucked the breath right out of him. He hadn't slept, hadn't eaten. If he was prone to drinking more than the occasional social glass, he'd have spent the last few days at the bottom of a bottle.

Although he was finding sleep deprivation was just as effective as alcohol in regards to numbing the mind.

"Would you at least shower?" Damian growled.

"Yeah, you're beginning to stink up the place, man." Adam slapped him on the back of the head.

The pair of them had been here all day. No matter what he said or didn't say, he couldn't get rid of them. Actually, now that he thought about it, at least one of his brothers had been with him twenty-four seven since he'd come home after quitting his job. What was up with that?

Not that he cared. They were pains in his ass and he'd keep on ignoring them.

"C'mon, Toby. You need to pull it together, man. A shower and clean clothes will make all the difference." Damian gave his shoulder a shove. "Toby?"

He couldn't summon the motivation to drag his ass off the couch. There was no way he was ready to make the distance from here to the bathroom. Lifting his head, he muttered, "Later."

"*Now.*" His mother breezed into the room. She walked over and grabbed him by the ear, gave it a twist. "Tobias Lachlan Moreland, if you don't hit that shower right now, I'll get your brothers to drag your sorry ass outside and I'll hose you off myself."

"Uh-oh, now you're in for it." Coop came into view. "Full name and a swear word."

Damian, Adam and Zac moved in beside Coop. Oh great. She'd brought the rest of the cavalry with her. "Mom..."

"What's the one thing I could give you that would make you feel better?" she asked, her fingers still tightly gripping his ear.

"Mad." There was no hesitation.

He knew he had to give Mad time, but fuck, it was killing him not being there for her while she sorted everything out at school. He'd spoken to Ted, through his lawyer at first, then himself this afternoon. He knew Mad had kept her job and, although Toby was no longer on staff, he would continue to coach the sports teams on a contract basis. But he needed to see her. See for himself that she was okay.

"You get in the shower right now and I promise you'll get exactly what you want."

Toby eyed his mother. She was up to something. "What did you do?"

Smiling, she let go of his ear and patted his cheek. "Wouldn't you like to know?"

"Yes, actually, I would." He blew out a breath. "She needs time."

"She's had plenty. And so have you." Grabbing the front of his shirt in her fist, she pulled him to his feet. "Shower. Now."

He let her direct him towards his room. They both knew she'd never be able to if he wanted to stand his ground. "Okay. I'm going."

"Finally." Adam threw up his hands. "Now can we stop babysitting duty?"

"Why are you all still here?" Mom asked, shooting one of her lethal glares at them.

Toby smiled and walked away to the sounds of his brothers' grumbles as their mother hustled them out of his house.

Memories assaulted him as he made his way through the bedroom into the bathroom. Mad was everywhere he looked. In the weeks they'd been together, she'd left pieces of her life all around his house. Clothes in his wardrobe, a toothbrush in his bathroom, her shampoo in the shower… The steamy space still smelled of her.

Taking a deep breath, Toby stripped out of his shirt and pants. Fuck. He had to see her. Would it be a dick move to park outside her house and wait for her to leave? To look through her windows with the hope of getting a glimpse?

He laughed. Knowing his luck, Damian would be the one to arrest him.

Flicking on the water, he stepped under the spray and let the shock of cold jolt him. It warmed quickly, and while he wanted to linger in this space that smelled of Mad, he didn't. He took care of the necessities quickly then shut the water off.

He'd promised himself he'd give her time but he didn't think he'd last much longer. Maybe he should get his mother to take all his keys so he couldn't drive over to Mad's house. Or he could go home to Mom and Dad's and hang out with them for the night. Get them to bring him back in the morning.

He grabbed a towel and slung it around his hips before heading back out to talk to his mother. He hadn't made it two steps into the bedroom when he froze.

Fuck.

It had finally happened. She'd lived up to her name and driven him mad. There was no other explanation for the apparition standing before him. He was hallucinating. He had to be. His sleep-deprived mind had conjured up his wildest dreams.

"Toby."

God, his imagination was so good, his vision even sounded like Mad.

"I used the key you gave me." She stood beside the bed, her hands twisting together in front of her in a nervous gesture he hadn't seen in a while. "I left it on—"

"Mad?" he shook his head. "You're real?"

"Ah, yes." Her head tipped to the side as she studied him. "Why wouldn't I be?"

"Jesus." Toby stalked over, gripped her arms and brought her to her toes. "Fuck. You're real."

"Toby—"

He slammed his mouth on hers. She melted instantly. Opened her mouth and welcomed him. And for the first time in seventy-two hours, he took a deep breath.

Pulling back, her pressed his forehead to hers. "You're real."

"You said that already."

"I know but I've been seeing you for days." He sighed. "You're never real."

"We need to talk."

"Need to touch you more." Toby started on the buttons of her blouse.

"Toby." She brushed his hands away. "Stop."

"No. Never." Pushing the shirt open, he sucked in a breath. "Damn. You and your sexy underwear."

"Toby." Mad wiggled out of his hold. "I've got things to say."

"I'm only hearing you if you're naked and pressed against me." He dropped his towel and stalked after her as she moved around the bed and headed for the door.

Lunging forward, he slid an arm around her waist and lifted her off her feet.

"Toby!"

"Madison!"

He spun around and dropped on the bed, making sure he didn't crush her when he came down on top. Framing her face with his hands, he stared at her, studied every millimeter of her face to see if she'd changed at all since he'd seen her.

"Christ. I finally get what Steve Tyler was singing about when he said he didn't want to miss a thing."

"What? Toby, you're not making any sense."

"Nothing makes sense when I don't have you."

She rolled her eyes. "Now you're being corny."

He shook his head. "Nope. It's the truth. I can't function without you, Mad."

"For god's sake, we've only been together a few weeks."

"I know." He held her gaze with his. "I think I was done the first time I kissed you."

"Done?"

"You're it for me. I don't get it. I can't explain it. But there it is. You're it." Her eyes filled with tear and his heart stopped.

"Dammit, Toby." She sniffed.

"Don't cry." He scrambled up, pulled her into his lap and tucked her head beneath his chin. "Whatever it is, whatever I said, I'll fix it. Just don't cry."

MADISON SUCKED back her tears and tried to swallow the lump in her throat. She needed to get the words out. Needed for Toby to shut up long enough for her to say the good stuff first.

"Don't cry. I'll fix it." He rocked her in his lap. "Mad, please, you're killing me."

Sniffling, she attempted to order her thoughts. "Can you shut up long enough for me to speak?"

Toby stopped rocking. "Ah, sure."

"Thank you."

"Always so polite," he murmured and held her tighter.

"Ease up, you're making it hard to breath."

His arms loosened. "Sorry."

"I'm mad at you." Madison covered his mouth with her hand to stop him from talking. "I'm allowed to be mad. You didn't give me a chance to make a decision about how we dealt with the debacle at school. I get that you're the alpha-male type and you thought you were doing what was right but if we're going to keep seeing each other, we have to meet halfway."

"What do you mean *if?*" he asked into her hand.

She lifted her hand away. "I wasn't sure..."

"Did you not hear one word I said?"

"Oh, I heard you. I'm still hearing you."

"What does that mean?"

"Everything is happening so fast and this is all new for me, remember."

Toby grabbed her hips and, picking her up, swung her around to straddle his lap. His very naked, very aroused lap. Forehead pressed to hers, he said, "This, with you, is new for me too. I've never told a woman I wasn't related to that I love her. Madison, I've held your hand through so many new experiences. I'm asking you to hold mine through this one."

He laid his hand open between them.

"Shit. Ignore that." He covered his cock with his other hand. "It can't be helped. You're in the room."

She knew he was being serious but hiding his erection behind his hand didn't stop her from shivering in anticipation.

He wiggled his fingers to bring her gaze back to the hand laid out in front of her. "Take my hand, Mad; share this new experience with me."

Her eyes filled once more. "I'm going to cry again."

Toby smiled. "As long as they're happy tears and you hold my hand while you do it, I'm okay with that."

Madison placed her hand on top of his. "Are we insane to fall in love this quickly?"

"Oh, it's definitely insane. Completely and utterly mad love."

EPILOGUE

"WHAT'S THIS?" Madison picked up the gift on her pillow.

"Birthday present."

"For me? My birthday was three months ago." She pulled the end of the pink ribbon to untie the bow.

"I know."

"You forgot to give it to me?" she asked while carefully lifting the tape from the paper so it didn't tear.

"No. You weren't ready then."

She glanced up. Toby leaned against the wall on the other side of his bedroom. They'd made the decision—today—to move in together, so she wondered what on earth he could be giving her other than the home he'd already offered.

"Hurry up."

Madison grinned. "I like to take my time. Anticipation's half the fun, right?"

"Not this time. I'm going to have a heart attack if you don't get a move on." He rubbed a hand over his chest. "Plus it's really hard staying all the way over here when you're all the way over there. Naked."

She'd just stepped out of the bathroom after a shower, which he hadn't joined her for. She should have known then something was up. The only time she showered alone in this house was when Toby wasn't home.

"C'mon, Mad, you're killing me."

She peeled back the paper to reveal more paper. Tissue paper this time. "What on earth?"

Giving up on slow, she tore into the final layers and watched as a delicate porcelain figurine was revealed. "Oh god."

Her gaze darted to Toby. He looked equally nervous and excited.

Glancing back down, she removed all the wrapping and held the couple cradled in her hands. "I don't—"

"Madison."

He was beside her. On one knee with his hand held out.

"Take this new experience with me."

In the palm of his hand sat a ring of gold, a big sparkly diamond the only thing breaking the circle. "Is that...? Are you...?"

Toby grinned. "I love it when I stop that mind of yours."

"It's only been five months."

"I told you I was done the first time I kissed you."

"I..." She couldn't take her eyes of the ring.

"In case you need the words... Madison, will you marry me?"

Her head was moving up and down before she could get a word out. "Y-yes."

"Then give me your hand."

She held out her left hand and watched him slip the gorgeous ring onto her finger.

"Right. Now, next new experience." He scooped her up into his arms and carried her out of the room.

"Wait. Where are we going?"

"I'm going to fuck my fiancé under the stars."

"Outside?"

"Yep."

"But—"

"And when I'm done, we're going to make slow, mad love."

If you enjoyed this book, please consider leaving a review. It only takes a few minutes and you'll be helping other readers find stories they'll enjoy, as well as supporting authors you love.

ABOUT THE AUTHOR

Rhian Cahill is the alter ego of a former stay-at-home mother of four. With motherly duties rapidly dwindling Rhian is able to make use of the fertile imagination she used to keep herself sane for all those years of slavery. Having spent years living overseas and visiting tropical climates has helped inspire some steamy stories.

Multi-published in erotic romance and contemporary romance, Rhian, with the help of Mr. Muse, spends her days and nights writing.

When not glued to the keyboard you'll find her book or knitting in hand avoiding any and all housework as much as possible.

For more on Rhian –

Website – http://www.rhiancahill.com/
Newsletter signup – http://eepurl.com/byrsf
Twitter – https://twitter.com/RhianCahill
FaceBook – https://www.facebook.com/RhianCahillAuthor
Instagram – http://instagram.com/rhiancahill/
BookBub – https://www.bookbub.com/authors/rhian-cahill
Goodreads page - https://www.goodreads.com/rhian_cahill

He needs to give his all or she'll accept nothing

A best friend's little sister story

Freddie Mann had the wildest night of her life with her brother's best friend, Zac Moreland. But instead of it leading to well, anything, it led to absolutely nothing. And that's just not on.

Zac Moreland knew he shouldn't act on the sizzling attraction between him Freddie. It was a dumb idea to risk a lifelong friendship with her brother over a one night stand. But Zac had long been a sucker for Freddie's charms and risk he did, only to learn that one night was never going to be enough, no matter how hard he tried to keep his distance.

Now, after months of doing everything in his power to avoid Freddie, Zac is ready to admit defeat and ask for mercy.

If only Freddie was feeling merciful. Her eyes are wide open where it comes to Zac and the faster he learns it's all or nothing the better.

http://www.rhiancahill.com/books/hearts-are-wild/no-more-talking/

He'll give her everything…if she dares to give him her heart

A reality really is better than fantasy story

Shaye Adams has thirty days to pack up her Sydney life and head across the country to her dream job in Perth. There's just one hot piece of unfinished business to take care of. Get Cooper Moreland into her bed and out of her system.

Coop couldn't be happier to be the man burning up Shaye's bed—except for the fact she insists it's a temporary, no strings arrangement with a firm end date. If he could just get Shaye to take off her blinders, she'd see that happiness was waiting for her right here in his arms.

As Shaye lives out every fantasy she's ever had about Coop, she realizes it's easy to hand over her body, but she never bargained for her heart going along for the wild ride. And now her biggest fear is the reality of Coop is better than any dream she's ever had.

http://www.rhiancahill.com/books/hearts-are-wild/dare-you-to/

LOOK FOR THESE TITLES BY RHIAN CAHILL

Party Games Series

Truth Or Dare

Spin The Bottle

Pass The Parcel – Novella

Are You Game Series

7 Minutes In Heaven – Book 1

Catch'n'Kiss – Book 2

Red Light, Green Light – Book 3

Hearts Are Wild Series

No More Talking (novella)

Dare You To (novella)

Mad Love

For a full list of Rhian's available books visit her website

http://www.rhiancahill.com/books/